# ULTRALIGHTS

# ULTRALIGHTS

## THE FLYING FEATHERWEIGHTS

### CHARLES COOMBS

ILLUSTRATED WITH PHOTOGRAPHS AND DIAGRAMS

WILLIAM MORROW AND COMPANY
New York • 1984

Photo Credits: Permission for photographs is gratefully acknowledged: American Aerolights Inc., pp. 7 (Don Monroe), 27 top, 47; Bill Baker, p. 137; Birdman Enterprises Ltd., p. 133; Cascade Ultralights, Inc., p. 19; CGS Aviation, p. 46; Cuyuna Engine Company, p. 38; Eipperformance Inc., pp. 3, 29 top, 76; Flight Designs, pp. 16, 17, 25, 57, 130, 131 both; Goldwing Ltd., pp. 134, 135 both; IBM Corp., p. 5; Maxair Sports, pp. II, 65; Pterodactyl Ltd., pp. 31, 129; Rockwell Corporation, p. 14; Rotec Engineering Inc., p. 27 bottom; Smithsonian Institution, p. 10; Ultralight Flight Inc., p. 106; United States Air Force, pp. 8, 13; U.S. Department of Commerce, p. 107 both; U.S. Department of Transportation, pp. 52, 54, 55, 60, 62, 122; Vector Aircraft Corp., p. 128. All other photographs by the author.

Library of Congress Cataloging in Publication Data
Coombs, Charles Ira, 1914-      Ultralights: the flying featherweights.
Bibliography: p.    Includes index. Summary: An introduction to a new, small, engine-powered, recreational aircraft and the sport, ultralighting, which it has generated. 1. Ultralight aircraft—Juvenile literature. [1. Ultralight aircraft] I. Title.   TL685.1.C66   1984      629.133'343
83-17411   ISBN 0-688-02775-X

# ACKNOWLEDGMENT

Most of us have occasional dreams in which, contrary to all the rules of aerodynamics, we take a few running steps, spread our arms and, presto, become airborne. We sail above the housetops, dodge between windblown trees, and, indeed, cavort with eagles.

Or else we long to have something like Mary Poppins's umbrella to transport us through the sky.

Well, the closest thing to it today is the smallest, engine-powered aircraft around—the ultralight. Designed by dreamers and put together with tubes, cables, and careful dedication, these machines have become familiar sights not only in the United States but in many other parts of the world.

Tracking down the makers and pilots of these unusual flying crafts was a most interesting and exciting experience for me. It was rewarding to meet with the instructors and to follow inexperienced students being put through their paces enroute to earning their wings. I found that ultralighters are a genial, co-operative, easy-to-talk-with group, and very willing to share their adventurous pastime with anyone interested.

I would like to thank the people at Eipperformance, Inc., Ultralight Flight, Inc., Goldwing, Inc., Birdman Enterprises, Ltd., Vector Aircraft Corporation, American Aerolights, Rotec Engineering, Inc., Flight Designs, Inc., Waspair, Pterodactyl, Ltd., Maxair Sports, and all others who generously provided me with data and illustrations.

The publishers of magazines and periodicals such as *Glider Rider, Ultralight Pilot,* and *Ultralight,* which are devoted specifically to ultralighting, also lent aid.

I am particularly indebted to two willing and enthusiastic allies who pitched in to help bring this book together. One is my son, Lee Coombs, whose darkroom wizardry made decent pictures out of my sometimes crude snapshots. The other is Bill Baker, an outstanding pilot and flying instructor who brought the whole subject to life before my wondering and sometimes startled eyes.

And to all of the many ultralighters who made the whole thing "take off," my many thanks.

Charles "Chick" Coombs
Westlake Village, California
1984

# CONTENTS

# 1. THE FUN OF FLYING

Ultralight flying is basically a throwback to the times when early-day airmen first began to realize their age-old dreams of sharing the sky with the birds. They took off in home-made, low-powered, wobbly machines made of sticks, wire, and cloth-covered wings. They had no instruments and little knowledge of aerodynamics. They simply flew by instinct—by the seat of their pants, as it came to be called. Their aim was primarily to experience the adventure of flying.

Now, almost a hundred years later, during which time aviation has developed and flourished beyond anyone's wildest imagination, there is a return to virtually the same style of flying that was thought to have been outgrown generations ago. Today men, women, boys, and girls are delighting in doing pretty much what their parents and grandparents did in the early days of manned flight. They are piloting low-flying, slow-moving, open-cockpit aircraft, called ultralights, which, like yesterday's pioneering machines, seem to have little more to offer than the proverbial "wing and a prayer."

For both lightness and strength, aluminum tubing has largely replaced the wooden stick construction so common to early aircraft. Stainless steel cable has proved superior to ordinary wire for holding everything together. Yet, all in all, the modern ultralight aircraft is about as slightly built and underweight as it can be and still carry a person safely into the sky. It is, in essense, a small, uncomplicated, inexpensive everyman's airplane, which provides the thrill and experience of powered flight in its utmost simplicity.

The sport of ultralighting started about a decade ago in the United States and quickly spread to many parts of the world. Since the craft requires neither licensing nor registration, there are no reliable records of how many are made and flown. But at this writing, there are estimates of more than 25,000 ultralights in the United States alone. Canada, Germany, England, France, Japan, and other nations account for added thousands. Ultralight manufacturing has become a multimillion-dollar industry that includes literally dozens of reputable producers of planes, products, and services. And with the growing ranks of enthusiasts already numbering in the hundreds of thousands,

An ultralight is the smallest powered manned aircraft in the sky.

Ultralighting is one of the fastest-growing outdoor sports around.

ultralighting is no more of a passing fancy than are sail-boating, motorcycling, skiing, sailboarding, or any of the other popular recreations that offer a fun-filled challenge.

The term "ultralight aviation" is relatively new and more ponderous than is necessary to describe such an un-complicated flying pastime. An ultralight is nothing more than the smallest, simplest, low-powered aircraft that is capable of transporting a person in flight. It could be called a minimum airplane, a miniplane, or even a teeny-plane. In Canada, England, Australia, and some European countries it is called a microlight. But by whatever name, the concept of ultralight aviation dates back to man's first attempts at powered flight.

In the late fifteenth and early sixteenth centuries, Leonardo da Vinci experimented with flapping-winged air machines, called ornithopters, that attempted to pattern their flight after that of birds. If he had succeeded, the first ultralight aircraft would have come into being some three hundred years before it actually did. But neither his machines nor those of many other early visionary aircraft builders were successful.

Leonardo da Vinci's birdlike ornithopter was a unique but unsuccessful idea for a man-powered flying machine.

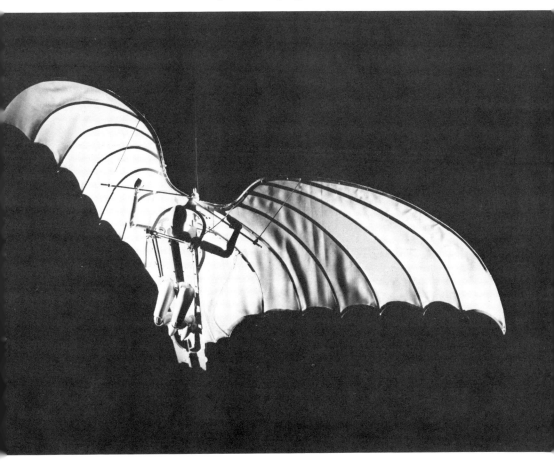

The main problem that plagued all early forms of manned flight was the lack of a sufficiently lightweight source of power to make the machine fly. Most early attempts were designed to use muscle power. But man's ambition and imagination far exceeded his actual strength. It has been calculated that a well-trained 175-pound person can generate a little less than ½ horsepower for a period of 5 to 30 minutes, depending upon that person's physical condition. This proved to be far less than the amount of energy needed to lift early-day flying machines off the ground, let alone sustain them aloft. (A most notable, modern exception occurred in 1979 when a young bicycle rider, Bryan Allen, literally pedaled a propeller-driven, filmy-winged aircraft into the sky and across the English Channel from Great Britain to France. Crossing over the watery 22¼ miles in 2 hours and 49 minutes, this man-powered flight of the *Gossamer Albatross* was an historic achievement indeed. In addition to Bryan Allen's strength and fortitude, the feat was made possible by employing twentieth-century computers and an intricate knowledge of engineering and aerodynamics, plus the use of new lightweight materials that were undreamed of a scant century ago.)

During the latter part of the nineteenth century, various aviation pioneers in different parts of the world abandoned

The muscle-powered *Gossamer Albatross* on its record-breaking English Channel crossing.

the idea of trying to manipulate flapping homemade wings. Instead they began giving proper attention to the four basic forces of aerodynamics that determine whether or not an object will fly—thrust, drag, lift, and gravity (or weight). If drag is stronger than thrust, and gravity overcomes lift, the craft will not take off. When thrust and lift predominate, the object is apt to fly.

First they built motorless aircraft that had rigid, or fixed, wings designed with curved surfaces to produce lift as they sped through the air. Having no suitable engines to generate thrust, there was no way the craft could get going and

Wind-borne gliders and sailplanes were subjects of early experiments in manned flight. This is a modern-day descendant.

take off from level ground. Rather, their makers carted them to the hilltops, launched them, and glided silently down into the valleys.

Such glider pioneers as England's Sir George Cayley, Otto Lilienthal of Germany, and Americans like Octave Chanute and the Wright brothers designed and flew homemade gliders that eventually led to powered aircraft. At least, man was successfully trying out his homemade wings.

During this time fairly lightweight gasoline-powered engines began to replace the cumbersome steam engines that were far too heavy to use in winged aircraft.

Wilbur and Orville Wright were quick to see such a gasoline engine as the answer to their dream of powered flight. Setting aside their gliders, they built a new flying machine and designed an engine that they hoped would provide enough power to lift the craft from the ground. The finished engine weighed approximately 140 pounds, quite heavy for the scant 12 horsepower it could generate. In order to gain the most thrust from their engine, they carved two carefully designed broad-bladed propellers out of slabs of spruce.

On December 17, 1903, from Kill Devil Hills, on the North Carolina coast near Kitty Hawk, Orville took his position lying belly-down across the biplane's lower wing. Grasping the flight-control levers, he revved the clattering powerplant. As they thrashed the air, the two large-bladed, pusher-type propellers set up a whomp-whomping sound that echoed across the windswept sand dunes.

Held back by a restraining wire, the frail aircraft trembled to be free. Orville glanced at Wilbur, who stood at the right wingtip trying to hold it steady. Taking a deep breath, Orville braced himself and released the holdback wire.

The machine trembled as though to shake apart. Then it began moving slowly down a special 60-foot guide track laid across the sand. Faster and faster it went, with Orville, white-knuckled, fearing that the straining engine would tear itself to pieces.

Running alongside, Wilbur finally gave up the chase

and stood staring, awestruck, as the machine wobbled and plunged ahead into the wind. Then the wooden, muslin-covered aircraft rose shakily from the track. It dipped dangerously toward the ground, then climbed again about 10 feet into the air. After traveling 120 feet in approximately 12 seconds, Orville eased the wondrous flying machine down to a skidding stop on the dune grass.

For the first time in history an airplane had raised itself with its own power and flown!

Before the day was over, the Wright brothers took turns at the controls and made three more flights. The final flight, piloted by Wilbur, lasted almost a minute and covered an amazing 852 feet.

Generally speaking, ultralighting began with the Wright brothers' first flight at Kitty Hawk.

No longer was aviation confined to gliders. The age of powered flight had arrived!

Although quite heavy by today's standards for featherweight recreational aircraft, the Wright *Flyer* can well be considered the first ultralight. Like an ultralight, it had fabric-covered wings and was braced with wire. It carried a minimum of instruments—only a revolutions-per-minute (rpm) engine-speed counter, a small wind-speed indicator, and a stopwatch. The pilot was fully exposed to the windstream. He helped guide the aircraft by moving a small stick forward or back to lower or raise the nose. He shifted his weight to keep the wings level or induce a turn, as is done to control some present-day ultralights.

In his swinglike harness, a young student learns how weight shifting helps control the ultralight's flight.

During the decade following Kitty Hawk, the flying
fever spread around the globe, particularly in America,
England, Russia, Germany, France, and Italy. Aircraft
manufacturing grew steadily into a worldwide industry.
However, as war became imminent, emphasis turned from
lightweight recreational aircraft to larger, heavier, and
more powerful airplanes that could carry guns and bombs.
The beginning era of what could be classified as ultralight
aviation ended abruptly.

During the years of the first World War, 1914 through
1918, enormous strides were made in aviation, but virtually all of the progress was war-oriented. High-powered
combat aircraft, both sprightly fighters and heavy multi-
engined bombers, filled the skies over Europe, helping to
win the war for the Allies.

After the Armistice, during the 1920s and 1930s, interest in military pursuits lessened, and civil aviation filled
the gap. Airplanes grew ever larger, more comfortable,
and highly sophisticated. Open cockpits disappeared. New
instruments were introduced into planes. Seat-of-the-pants
flying became a forgotten art. As aviation became a gigan-
tic business, the simple airplane developed into a massive
passenger and cargo-carrying airliner. Scheduled air routes
stretched between the nation's major cities, and, indeed,
traced new trails around the world.

As typified by the World War I Spad, early aircraft quickly grew into larger, more powerful war machines.

Although there was still occasional talk about "a plane in every garage," very little attention actually was given to small, single-seat airplanes that might be classified as ultralights.

During World War II (1938–1945), planes grew still more powerful, faster, and infinitely more complex. At the very end of the war, military jet aircraft made a brief appearance in European skies.

Significantly, the jet age began shortly after the war. Soon giant airliners such as the Boeing 707 and later the

The age of the jet emerged from World War II. This is one of the
U.S. Air Force's F86F Sabre jets.

mammoth 747s flew global routes carrying millions of passengers to all parts of the world. Anyone who thought small in this era of bigness was out of step with the times. Or so it seemed.

Yet, there was a widely scattered but growing group of young men and women who felt that the real joys of flying were being lost in giant aircraft crowded with hundreds of people having drinks and watching movies in air-conditioned splendor at altitudes of 30,000 feet or more. Flying had become a business, no longer geared to produce pleasure or adventure. This group of enthusiasts set out to recapture the fun and thrills of flying in small aircraft where they could hear the propeller sounds, feel the wind in their faces, and have the controls at their fingertips.

Some of them went back to building lightweight gliders or sailplanes. Long-winged, stiffly structured affairs, these aircraft were usually difficult to store and transport. Besides, they had to be launched from a hilltop or slope, or be towed aloft by a powered plane. Enjoyable though it was, glider flying was extremely limited in scope.

Around 1960 an aeronautical researcher named Francis Rogallo developed a lightweight, plastic, arrowhead-shaped, flexible wing called a parasail or parawing. It was originally meant to be used as a gliding type of parachute

Hang gliders developed from the simple parasail-type wing.

for lowering pieces of cargo or equipment gently to the ground from high-flying aircraft.

The Rogallo parawing was never adopted by the military for which it was intended. But some young gliding enthusiasts tried it out. They rigged up a sort of trapeze on which they could hang beneath the outspread fabric of the ribless wing. With the aid of a few wires, they controlled the flight by subtly shifting their weight on the trapeze.

The sport of hang gliding was born. It continues to flourish.

However, it was inevitable that someone eventually would think of adding power to a hang glider, thus turning it into an airplane of minimum sorts. In the mid-1970s, assorted hang-gliding experts began experimenting by adding a small gasoline engine and a propeller to their craft. They used any lightweight engine they could find, taking them off of snowmobiles, go-carts, chainsaws, lawn mowers, or adapting old outboard motors. Almost any lightweight engine could be and was used.

Since a hang glider did not have wheels and a landing gear, the flyer simply opened the throttle, ran a few steps

Adding power, landing wheels, and a place to sit turns a hang glider into an ultralight plane.

into the wind, and took off. Similarly, he landed on his feet, letting the aircraft settle around him. The process was called foot-launching. Foot-launching was incorporated into most early ultralights and actually helped them to share an official classification with hang gliders rather than with standard, landing-gear-equipped airplanes. Thus, as with hang gliders, they did not have to be registered or their pilots licensed by the Federal Aviation Administration (FAA).

In the late seventies, ultralight designs changed dramatically. Instead of raglike parasails, some designers began using ribbed and strutted wings. Elementary fuselages tipped with rudders and elevators were added for more positive control during flight. Many ultralights featured seats rather than slinglike harnesses to support the pilot. Ultralights began to look more like airplanes than hang gliders, although some had strange shapes. In all cases, emphasis was on minimum size, weight, and cost, plus maximum safety, simplicity, and portability. As these criteria were approached, and public interest was heightened, the number of ultralight aircraft began increasing enormously. Ultralighting took off, as it were.

Today, on any calm morning or in the twilight hours of dusk, the air sometimes seems filled with oversized, rain-

bow-hued butterflies weaving about the sky, albeit some-
what loudly. On close inspection they are seen to be tiny
piloted aircraft. Not only are they fun to fly, but, like butterflies, they are colorful and environmentally safe. They
don't scar the land, pollute streams, or damage fragile en-
vironments. They are small, portable, and easy to maintain. Compared to other types of powered aircraft, they are
quite inexpensive.

They are the ultralights, a new and exciting generation
of easy-to-fly recreational airplanes.

For fun and adventure, ultralights have found their spot in the field
of recreational activity.

# 2. THE MACHINES

For a while the accepted standard that separated an ultralight from a regular airplane was its capability of being foot-launched by the pilot, running into the wind to assist in the takeoff, and by landing on his or her feet. Since the craft had no landing gear, it could not really be called an airplane. Like a hang glider, it escaped many of the rules, regulations, and FAA licensing requirements that applied to airplanes.

But as ultralights developed, wheels began to appear on them. Running takeoffs and landings went out of style. The question then arose of whether or not the vehicle was simply a powered hang glider, or whether it had developed to the point where it should be classified as an airplane. Since ultralights had to share the sky with other flying vehicles, some kind of ruling was needed concerning their proper place in aviation.

In 1982, after long discussions, ultralight manufacturers

and flyers convinced the FAA that they could conduct and regulate themselves in a safe and sane manner.

Despite a willingness to give ultralighters the opportunity for self-government, the FAA did establish a few standards for determining whether the craft was an ultralight, and therefore not needing registration and certification, or an airplane. No longer, the FAA ruled, are foot-launching and -landing capabilities the basis for an ultralight classification. Rather, to be regarded as an ultralight the aircraft cannot weigh more than 254 pounds (115 kilograms) empty. It cannot hold more than one person. It can carry no more than 5 gallons of fuel. Its maximum speed cannot exceed 55 knots (63 miles per hour). For the sake of safety it must not stall or lose its ability to remain in flight at any speed of more than 24 knots (approximately 27½ mph). For all intents and purposes, the aircraft is to be used only for sport and recreational purposes.

Provided with basic guidelines, a host of manufacturers began producing or modifying ultralights to fit the FAA standards. Many marginal ultralight builders were unable to meet the specifications and dropped by the wayside. New ones popped up. Most of those that still survive do so by putting out a durable, well-tested, safe machine. It is pretty much up to the flyer or purchaser to study and in-

Ultralights come in a variety of shapes.

spect various ultralights carefully to determine which one is best suited to his or her needs.

After determining what type of craft you want, you may decide to purchase a hundred-dollar or so set of plans and building instructions for a particular ultralight. You would then have to gather the materials necessary to make the machine on your own. This is a challenging way to do it, and those willing to tackle the task must be quite skilled and have the proper tools to work with. They must also know their way around metal supply houses, lumberyards, hardware stores, and numerous other sources of materials. Building from blueprints is for the skilled and knowledge-able craftsman.

More common than blueprints are kits provided by the manufacturer. Kits usually cost upwards of two thousand dollars and often contain more than a thousand precut parts shipped in several boxes. The buyer need only follow detailed instructions for putting the ultralight together so it looks and flies like the pictures in the manual. Often some of the more complex assemblies are put together at the factory before they are shipped. Assembling an ultralight from a kit demands a considerable amount of a model-maker's patience and skill with basic tools, but often it is worth both the challenge and savings in money.

Assembling an ultralight can be an exacting task.

The third, and most costly, way to get an ultralight is to purchase a fully assembled model from a dealer. Although the $3000 to over $7000 price for an airworthy craft is expensive, it can be more affordable if you and several enthusiasts, or members of a club, band together to share both the pleasures and the expenses involved in ultralighting. With a readymade craft you will need to learn how to unfold it or break it down to its major parts so that, in the interest of portability, you can trailer it or wrap it up and carry it on a cartop. You must also learn to put the main assemblies back together properly when you want to fly. Depending upon the aircraft, assembly or disassembly may take from a few minutes to about an hour.

There are many radically different designs of ultralight aircraft. However, there are basic major parts common to most all of them. There is a fuselage and at least one wing, often called a *sail*. There is a power package of one or more engines. There are rudders, ailerons, elevators, or other types of movable surfaces by which the aircraft can be guided, plus the controls to operate them. Each part, of course, must work in close harmony with all the others in order for the flying entity to become efficient and safe to operate.

The fuselage of an ultralight bears little resemblance to that of a standard airplane. It is often no more than a rigid

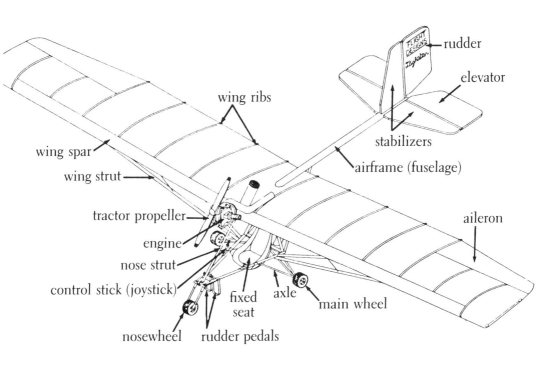

Basic ultralight parts.

backbone, or keel, that serves to anchor the wing, tail, engine, and other parts of the aircraft. It may be a piece of tempered aluminum tubing, a square beam of thin strong steel, or even a length of plastic irrigation pipe. Or the fuselage may be made up of a framework composed of one

An ultralight may use a simple length of metal or plastic pipe as its fuselage, or keel.

or more triangle-shaped pieces of tubing. Triangles are popular, since they are the basic shape for strong rigid construction.

Included in the fuselage or attached to it are the landing-gear assembly and the pilot's seat. The landing gear may be a tricycle-type with two main wheels, generally called "mains," and one nosewheel. Or the aircraft may be a tail-dragger type, with two mains and a simple tailskid or tailwheel; this was very common to early-day aircraft. Many landing gears are so designed that they can be changed to pontoons or skis when water or snow operations are desired.

(Left) Tricycle landing gears are most popular.

(Below) Many ultralights convert easily to pontoon planes.

The so-called cockpit of an ultralight can be a simple hammock-like sling that allows the pilot to shift his or her weight around in order to help control the aircraft. Or it can be a solidly anchored seat if the aircraft uses actual steering controls instead of the weight-shift method.

As with all parts of an ultralight, the airframe must be kept as lightweight as possible without unduly sacrificing strength. Thus, instead of an abundance of heavy struts and solid wood or metal bracings, many ultralights use a web of stainless steel cables to strengthen the assembly. These cables play a particularly important role in supporting the wing both from above and below.

Cable-supported ultralights usually have a king post that thrusts straight up from the center of the wing. Cables attached to the tip of the post stretch downward and outward to the wingtips and other parts of the aircraft that need support. Other thin cables may angle upward from the landing-gear area to brace the underside of the wing and also uphold the tail surfaces, or empennage.

The numerous ultralights that do not use support cables utilize solid trusses or heavier bracing. The wing is constructed around a solid tip-to-tip spar.

Most ultralights have a single wing, although a few biplanes are being made. Having largely been patterned after

(Above) King post and cable bracing are commonly used in ultralights.
(Below) Even biplanes have entered the ultralight field.

flexible hang-glider wings, many ultralight wings are made of a single thickness of fabric, similar to the sail on a small boat or a windsurfer's sailboard. Usually made of strong, closely woven, rip-resistant Dacron material, the ultralight single-surfaced wing is designed and stitched to fit over a lightweight spar stretching along the front, or leading, edge of the wing. Batten pockets similar to those used on a boat sail are spaced along the rear, or trailing, edge of the wing. Specially curved metal ribs slip into these

A single-surfaced wing generally uses specially bent rods to stiffen it and give it an aerodynamic contour.

pockets to stiffen the wing and give it an essential airfoil shape. This type of flexible wing is easy to assemble and dismantle.

Another type of wing is double-surfaced. It is constructed much like the wing of a standard airplane. That is, it is made up of carefully designed built-up ribs and spars around which the wing fabric is wrapped and permanently attached. The upper and lower shape of the wing differ and have a more efficient aerodynamic shape than a single-surfaced wing that has the same curvature on both top and bottom surfaces.

Fabric wrapped over and under a series of ribs provides the Pterodactyl Ascender a double-surfaced wing.

Some ultralights roll up into a neat package.

But due to its more detailed construction, the double-surfaced wing cannot simply be taken apart, rolled up, or tucked away. About the best that can be done is to fold the two halves back along the fuselage, or detach and slip them into a trailer alongside the rest of the aircraft. Despite its being less portable, the strong double-surfaced, rib-braced wing does not normally need much in the way of cables or other braces to maintain strength and rigidity.

Some double-surfaced wings even have adjustable built-in slots or flaps. When the slots are in open position, or when the flaps are lowered, the airflow is changed and the aircraft does not stall at slow speed so readily. By delaying stalls as well as adding lift to the wing, they enable the aircraft to land at reduced speed.

Either type of wing may also have ailerons along its trailing edge. Ailerons are wing tabs that move opposite to each other. One tips up as the one on the opposite wingtip tilts down when the control stick is moved from side to side. By deflecting a portion of the airstream, they cause the wing to tip one way or the other. When worked in combination with a rudder, the use of ailerons produces properly banked turns.

In the absence of ailerons there may be spoilerons, or spoilers, located on the top of the wing, one on each side. The spoiler is simply a small-hinged rectangular barrier that may be sewed to the fabric or attached with Velcro fasteners. Controlled from the cockpit, when one spoiler is tilted up into the windstrem it disrupts the airflow, and therefore reduces the lift generated along that section of the wing. With less lift, that side of the wing drops lower, thus rolling or banking the plane into a turn very much in the manner normally accomplished with ailerons.

The tail surfaces, called the empennage, can be grouped along with the main wing. Usually the empen-

A conventional empennage features movable rudder and elevators attached to fixed vertical and horizontal stabilizers.

nage is made up of a vertical rudder and a horizontal stabilizer. The rudder, of course, steers the plane to left or right, or causes it to yaw sideways. The stabilizer steadies the plane in level flight. Along the trailing edge of the stabilizer there is usually an elevator, a simple up-and-down moving vane that tilts or pitches the aircraft up or down to put it into a climb or dive. At times the empennage assembly is shaped like a V or Λ, with slanting rudders and attached elevators. These so-called "ruddervators" serve the same purposes as do the more common horizontal and vertical tail surfaces.

But not all ultralights have a trailing empennage. Some are controlled by a small canard wing that sticks out in front of the plane. The canard probably has an elevator attached for pitch control. With a canard, the familiar rear end rudder may be missing. Instead, there may be small vertical surfaces, or drag rudders, stuck out on each of the craft's wingtips.

A forward canard wing plus vanes on tips of the main wing control a tailless ultralight.

Variety is the spice of ultralighting: The aircraft may have one wing or two. Its wing may resemble that of a bat, a kite, a sailplane, or even a miniature airliner. Rudders and elevators can be at the rear of the aircraft, in front, or, indeed, absent altogether.

Often a hang-glider owner, in order to extend his flying capabilities, may add a trike to his craft. A trike is a framework containing a landing gear, seat, and engine. Thus, with a trike assembly hung beneath it, a hang glider is converted to a powered ultralight.

A trike converts a hang-glider wing into a powered ultralight.

The power package that lifts an ultralight into the sky and keeps it flying consists primarily of an engine and a propeller, to which are added a fuel system, switch, and throttle. Almost any lightweight, ten- to thirty-horsepower gasoline-fuel unit can be adapted to turn a propeller. Most such engines, from chainsaw to lawn mower types, are of the two-cycle variety. In a two-cycle engine the spark plug fires each time the piston reaches the top of its stroke, driving it back down in the cylinder. The up-and-down action is geared to turn a propeller shaft. The two-cycle

An ultralight engine is a compact power package.

ultralight engine normally has one or two cylinders, de-pending upon how much power is desired.

Unless equipped with a proper muffler, the rapid-firing two-cycle engine is noisy. It burns a mixture of gasoline laced with small amounts of oil that keeps it lubricated while it is running. Ultralighters usually mix their own fuel according to engine specifications. At full throttle the

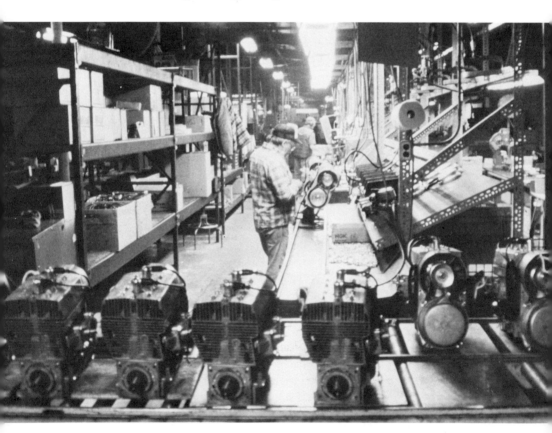

An ultralight-engine assembly line is small but busy.

engine usually operates at an excessive speed of between 6,000 and 7,000 rpm's. At such high engine rpm's the tips of the spinning propeller blades approach the speed of sound. This induces a turbulence that creates drag and diminishes propeller thrust. So the ultralight may use a system of belt drives or mechanical gearing to reduce the high direct-drive engine-shaft speed to about a 3,000 rpm propeller speed. This is about right for maximum thrust. The reduced rpm's also cut down on the noise produced by high-speed prop tips.

However, instead of reduction gears or pulleys, some direct-drive engines use a small propeller turning at high speed. Such propellers are extremely noisy and less efficient than larger props operating at reduced rpm's, but they are used because of their simplicity and lightness.

The propeller often is mounted behind the engine, making it a pusher-type aircraft. If mounted forward of the engine to pull the plane, the aircraft is called a tractor-type.

The props usually are carved of laminated hardwoods, although other materials such as plastic compounds, metal, nylon, or fiberglass sometimes are used. The leading edges of nonmetal blades often are rimmed with a metallic or other hard substance to reduce the risk of nicking by gravel or other flying objects.

Laminated hardwood propellers are used in many ultralights.

Keeping the power pack of engine, rpm-reduction gearing, and propeller shaft as lightweight as possible is all-important. Approximately thirty pounds is about as lightweight as can be managed, and most weigh more.

Most engines are started with a pull cord, although a few use electric starters. The T-handle of the starter cord is mounted within easy reach of the seated pilot. This is essential for in-flight re-starting in case the engine should die unexpectedly.

Although ultralights are allowed to carry as much as five gallons of fuel, normally smaller, two- to four-gallon tanks are used to keep down weight. They are attached in as safe and out-of-the-way a place as possible. Since motor size and tank size vary with individual ultralights, their flight ranges also vary. Generally, however, an ultralight will consume from less than a gallon to about a gallon and a half of fuel per hour and travel some thirty to fifty miles in doing so.

Rounding out the ultralight aircraft are the controls by which the plane is flown and the instruments by which the pilot is made aware of how the plane is acting and what it is doing.

As with most other facets of the activity, there is no standard method for controlling an ultralight. A hang-glider pilot often hangs suspended in a free-swinging trapeze or harness and guides the craft by shifting his or her weight forward and aft or from side to side. This puts pressure on cables stretching from the harness to various control surfaces that steer the glider. Logically, this is called *weight-shifting*. Sometimes this method is used in the small flexible-winged ultralights. Often weight-shifting combines with joystick and rudder-bar-operated aerodynamic controls for more positive steering.

Many ultralights, however, have a fixed pilot's seat and don't rely on shifting body weight. They use some variation of the joystick and rudder-pedal-control system that is common to standard airplanes.

An ultralight cockpit featuring (A) a fixed seat, (B) control stick with (C) attached brake handle, and (D) a handy post-mounted throttle.

By using aerodynamic controls, plus manipulation of the throttle, the ultralight pilot maintains mastery over the craft.

The ultralighter probably has a few instruments to help determine whether or not he or she is doing things safely and properly. The instruments may be fastened to various sections of the cockpit tubing within easy view of the pilot. Or they may be clustered together in a neatly enclosed package mounted in front of or beside the pilot.

Although an experienced ultralight pilot may be able to fly by the seat of the pants, as it were, one's senses are far from foolproof. An airspeed indicator (ASI) is an important aid to all flyers, including the veteran. By glancing at it, the pilot can keep the aircraft speed well below the maximum for which it was designed and prevent overstraining its capacity. The ASI also indicates when speed falls to the point of approaching a dangerous stall as well as helps to maintain the best cruising speed for fuel economy. The airspeed indicator may be a clocklike instrument with a needle and dial to indicate miles per hour. However, many ultralight aircrafts use a less complicated wind meter which is a simple calibrated tube with a disc that is moved up and down by the pressure of air velocity striking it.

In a simple wind meter, air rams through a small hole to raise a disk up or down a miles-per-hour scale.

Another instrument, an altimeter, is needed to keep the pilot informed on how high he or she is. Small altimeters are available that can be strapped to the arm like a wristwatch. The more common, and probably more accurate, altimeters are clocklike devices on which numerals appear marking 100-foot intervals of height.

Many ultralighters include a magnetic compass in their instrument package, although it is sometimes considered excess baggage. Pilots of slow-flying, low altitude, short-range ultralight aircraft travel mostly by line of sight reckoning. They follow local maps or such familiar landmarks as roads, rivers, railroads, ridges, or highly visible power lines. This method of navigation is called *pilotage*.

A neat cluster of uncomplicated and helpful ultralight instruments.

Yet, a compass is a very desirable aid for cross-country flying over unfamiliar terrain and for following the directions indicated on government sectional charts, the detailed maps commonly used for aerial navigation.

Due to the extra weight and the fact that ultralights usually stay away from tower-controlled airports, radios are seldom used.

For engine care a tachometer keeps track of the rpm's and helps the pilot prevent overstraining the engine and causing excessive wear. An engine temperature gauge helps avoid overheating.

There are an infinite number of ways that the major components such as airframe, wing, engine, control sur-

faces, and instruments can be put together to make an
ultralight aircraft. Some have high wings, some low.
Some have more than one wing; some more than one engine. Some are pushers; some are pullers. In most ultralights the pilot sits exposed to the windstream and claims
that is part of the fun. A few have partially enclosed cockpits, but their pilots seem to have just as much fun despite
the additional comfort.

The added comfort of an enclosed cockpit appeals to some
ultralighters.

A two-seater, though not legally an ultralight, can be used for training purposes.

By far, most ultralights are single-place machines. Yet, there are some two-place ultralights. They are frequently used in the teaching of student fliers. When operated by a certified pilot for instruction purposes, these dual-control crafts, similar to the single-seaters, need not be licensed. However, if they are used for conventional passenger-carrying functions, the two-seaters must be properly certified and registered by the FAA as a regular aviation aircraft.

However, regardless of the type, as long as the aircraft complies with the basic design and performance regulations as set up by the Federal Aviation Administration and widely accepted by manufacturers and fliers alike, the vehicle is considered to be an ultralight . . . an unusual aircraft that brings back the sheer fun and excitement of powered flight in its simplest form.

# 3. GROUNDWORK

Any man or woman, boy or girl, regardless of age, who is reasonably sound of body and mind, has a fair share of natural ability, and is willing to devote some time and effort to the cause can learn to fly an ultralight aircraft. This is part of the appeal of ultralighting, for it is often a group affair where members of a family or club learn and train together and, when ready, take their turns flying the plane.

But that turn will not come easily. It must be earned through study and hard work. And for good reason. Whenever you leave the ground you take on extra risk. To a degree the risk increases with height, although plunging to earth from an altitude of five thousand feet is scarcely more damaging than crashing from a hundred feet. So it is not only prudent but extremely critical to your safety and enjoyment that you prepare yourself with knowledge and training similar to that which any student aviator would

Ultralighting attracts spectators.

undergo, so you will be aware of what you are doing before your feet leave the ground.

Although there are no size, age, or physical restrictions for pilots, no required licenses, or firm standards of training, the FAA also strongly recommends thorough ground and flight training before a person attempts to solo an ultralight. This is simply common sense—or survival, if you wish. Most reliable ultralight dealers will not sell an aircraft unless the purchaser agrees to a course in preflight and flying training. Nor can someone rent one until the dealer has first checked out the applicant to be sure he or she has been properly trained and has some flying experience. Any person who builds an ultralight from a set of plans, or a kit of parts, would be most foolish not to take proper training before attempting to fly his or her home-built craft.

When learning to pilot an ultralight, first you should know something about what makes the aircraft fly. This is called *aerodynamics*, the science of flight within the earth's atmosphere.

Aerodynamics deals with four forces—thrust, drag, lift, and gravity—and how each works. Actually, they tend to work pretty much against each other. The forces of lift and gravity are in a constant tug-of-war. While lift tries to make the aircraft rise, gravity tugs to keep it or bring it down. If the craft is standing still, gravity wins, and its wheels remain firmly on the ground.

However, when the plane moves forward at a fast enough speed, the flow of air over and under its specially designed wing increases the pressure on the underside and creates a vacuum over the curved top. With positive pressure pushing from below and negative pressure, or a vacuum, offering no resistance from above, the wing rises upward. And, since the rest of the ultralight, including the seat with you in it, is attached to the wing, up you go too. As long as the upward lift equals or exceeds the downward pull of gravity, you will stay up.

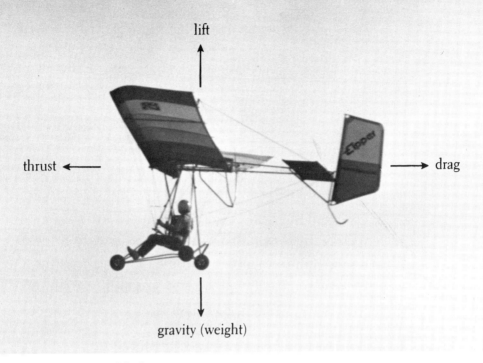

lift

thrust

drag

gravity (weight)

The four forces of flight.

Now, in a fixed-wing aircraft, which includes all ultralights and all familiar jet and propeller-driven airplanes,
some force is required to get the vehicle moving forward
fast enough so the air passing over the wing produces
enough lift to raise it. This brings into play the other pair
of forces—thrust and drag. Quite simply, thrust is the
power unit that pulls or pushes the aircraft forward. In an
ultralight this is invariably an engine or two with propellers attached. It doesn't matter whether the propeller is
mounted up front to pull the craft or is located to the rear

to push it. The propeller is still producing thrust—the energy needed to generate forward momentum.

On the other hand, the friction of the air against surfaces of the aircraft tends to hold it back. The wind that blows against your cheeks or whistles through the wire rigging also slows the craft. This resistance to forward motion is called drag. If the thrust is stronger than the drag, the aircraft will move forward. If drag is stronger, say the engine and prop are too small to be effective, you will stay put. Or at least you will not be able to build up enough forward speed to generate sufficient lift over the wing to make the plane rise.

In studying aerodynamics you find there are ways to

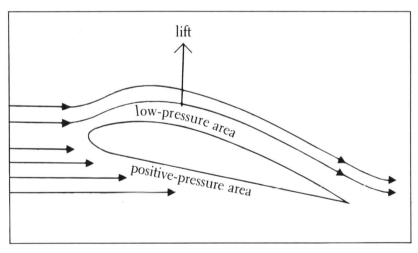

Wing shape and airspeed help produce lift.

help make lift overcome gravity, and enable thrust to free the craft from drag's sticky fingers. Of course, the best solution in either case is to have plenty of power. The more power your plane has, the less dependent the vehicle is on wings that are shaped for high degrees of lift. With enough power or thrust aimed in an upward direction, the craft doesn't even need wings. It becomes a rocket. But that possibility doesn't really interest an ultralight pilot.

Usually extra power means extra engine weight. And remember, the total empty weight of an ultralight cannot exceed 254 pounds. Even with the limited power that all ultralights must contend with, the pilot can increase lift by tilting the wing upward a bit as it reaches takeoff velocity. This increased tilt is called the *angle of attack*. By increasing the angle of attack you increase the pressure of the wind hitting the underside of the wing. At the same time you generate more vacuum atop the wing. Thus additional lift is obtained.

But the angle of attack has to be carefully controlled. If the wing is pitched up too steeply—too much angle of attack—the wing becomes like a barn door facing into the wind. It not only fails to produce lift but causes drag to the extent that the aircraft may lose its flying speed, stall, and crash.

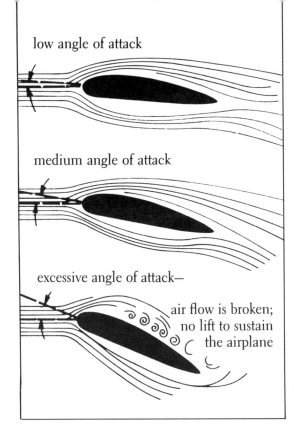

low angle of attack

medium angle of attack

excessive angle of attack—

air flow is broken;
no lift to sustain
the airplane

Angle of attack may increase lift or produce a dangerous stall.

The skilled manipulation of the four forces of flight comes later with training and practice on a real aircraft. In ground school it is important that you first learn the theory behind lift, gravity, thrust, and drag—what they are and generally what they do.

In ground school you also learn that flight is controlled by rotating the aircraft in three separate directions, or around three so-called axes. These axes of rotation are referred to as *yaw, pitch,* and *roll.*

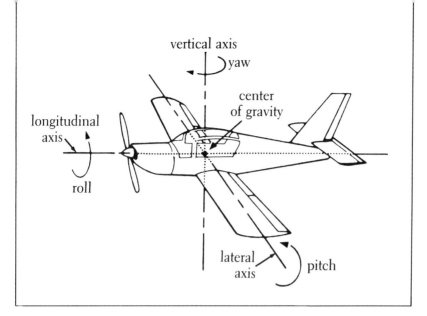

The three axes around which all flying movements rotate.

Yaw is a sort of side-to-side wagging of the tail. It is normally controlled by a rudder, which acts in the same manner as the rudder of a boat. On ultralights the rudder usually is activated by a foot bar or pedals.

Pitch is moving the nose up or down to climb or descend. In an aircraft pitch is normally achieved through movement of the elevator that is manipulated by the control stick, or joystick. If you push the joystick forward the elevator swings downward on its hinges. This deflects the airstream down, causes the tail to lift, and pitches the nose down. If you pull the stick back, the opposite action takes place, and the nose tilts skyward.

The elevator in a forward-located canard wing reacts

just the opposite, tilting down for a climb and up for a
dive.

The third axis around which a plane revolves is roll.
Just as it indicates, roll is the action of spinning around an
imaginery line that stretches lengthwise from the front to
the back of an aircraft. Generally, but again, not always,
for ultralights come in many strange and unusual designs,
roll is accomplished by use of a pair of ailerons located
along the trailing edge of each wing. The ailerons usually
are manipulated by sideways movements of the same control stick that operates the elevator. Both ailerons move at
the same time, but in opposite directions. As one tilts up,
the other dips down. If the left aileron moves up into the
airstream, pushing the wingtip down, and the right one
moves down, pushing that wingtip up, the aircraft rolls to
the left. And vice versa for a right roll.

In practice, a skilled pilot maneuvers the aircraft by carefully coordinating movement of the controls to combine
yaw, pitch, and roll smoothly to produce a climbing turn, a
change of direction to dodge around a cloud, or to sideslip
the plane while making a crosswind landing. Every movement is made according to the science of aerodynamics that
deals with the control of forces.

Having learned at least basic aerodynamics, before at-

This ultralight is equipped with conventional controls including rudder, elevators, and ailerons.

tempting to fly you should know something about the "stuff" you will be flying in—the air, or atmosphere. If air were just the lightweight, tasteless, odorless, colorless static material it is reputed to be, you would have no problem. But air is constantly moving, changing temperature, increasing or decreasiing in density, and otherwise stirring up potential problems for the flyer trying to steer a smooth course through it. The science of weather activity is called *meteorology*.

Meteorology is a broad subject that affects many phases of your life. It pretty much dictates whether you should put on a jacket or wear a pair of cut-off jeans before you leave the house. It tells you when to carry an umbrella and when to wax your skis. At the moment, however, you are concerned with how the changing weather affects flying an ultralight aircraft. Weather can be a valuable ally, or a deadly enemy.

You should learn about winds and clouds and how they are related. You need to be able to read the signs that indicate probable changes in the weather, particularly whether the change will be for better or for worse.

Bear in mind, however, that flying an ultralight is strictly a fair-weather activity. These low-powered, light-weight, relatively flimsy aircraft simply are not made for rough weather. Even with a fairly mild breeze of, say, fifteen or so knots, you are wise to remain on the ground. As for flying in the rain, don't even consider it. Not only is it usually an unsafe practice, but there is no pleasure to be had from sitting out in the open and being soaked by a cold driving rain.

During a basic study of meteorology you learn how different atmospheric conditions affect your craft. Level, warm air is less dense than cold air and provides less lift for an aircraft's wing. Warm air also has more moisture in it than crisp, clear, cold air, which cuts down on visibility. Yet, because you are quite exposed to the elements in an ultra-light, flying on a warm day is definitely preferable to flying on a cold one. The small difference in the amount of lift is not very important. You should be more concerned with possible winds, rain, or other weather changes.

Clouds are dependable indicators of weather changes. They mark potential hazards. Usually, low layers or sheets of clouds, known as *stratus*, indicate smooth air near the ground and favorable flying conditions. Even though you may not be able to see the sun because of the cloud layer, the air under the cloud cover is generally stable. There is little likelihood of rain falling from a layer of stratus.

On the other hand, when the sky fills with patches of puffy clouds, known as *cumulus*, an active change in weather is on its way. The increase in atmospheric moisture that forms the clouds indicates that a mass of warm air is starting to mix with a similar mass of cold air and condensing to form vapor. The same thing happens when you take a hot shower in a cold bathroom and the room fills with a cloud of steam.

If the cumulus clouds remain white, puffy, and move slowly like a flock of sheep nibbling across the sky, the air should remain reasonably quiet and good for flying. But when the edges of faster moving fronts of warm and cold

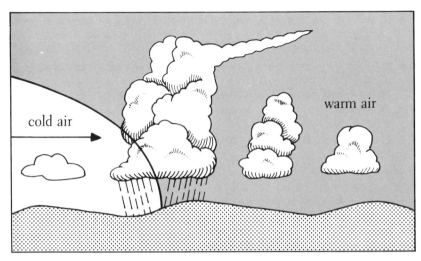

The collision of cold and warm air masses generates weather changes.

air masses collide, they are apt to generate winds and turbulence.

The cumulus clouds may thicken and become more ragged than puffy. Often called *cumulus fractus,* such gathering cloud masses signal increasing weather disturbances.

When the clouds build up into churning, darkly forbidding masses, you can count on high winds nearby and probably rain. These are *nimbus* clouds, and nimbus means rain. When they are low like a stratus cloud, they are called *nimbostratus,* and these also bring rain with them.

But the most imposing, dramatic, and dangerous clouds are the high-climbing, power-filled, cumulus type called *cumulonimbus*. Billowing, ever-churning, towering masses, the cumulo nimbus are filled with rain, hail, lightning, and cyclonic winds. They are to be avoided at all cost. Even to venture near such thunderheads is to risk being sucked into their deadly maelstrom.

Since you should avoid threatening changes of weather when flying an ultralight, a basic knowledge of meteorology is important, so you know what to look for in order to anticipate them.

Billowing thunderheads must be strictly avoided.

In ground school you learn about the action of air currents and winds. Both can affect the flight of your craft. Air currents can be either warm or cold. These are known as *convection currents*, since they are conveyed, or convected, off of various objects. Warm currents rise from warm objects. A field of freshly plowed dark earth absorbs heat from the sun. The heat rises, causing thermal activity. A thermal is sometimes capped by a puffy, flat-bottomed cumulus cloud that forms when the rising warm and cold upper air meet. You can take advantage of a ris-

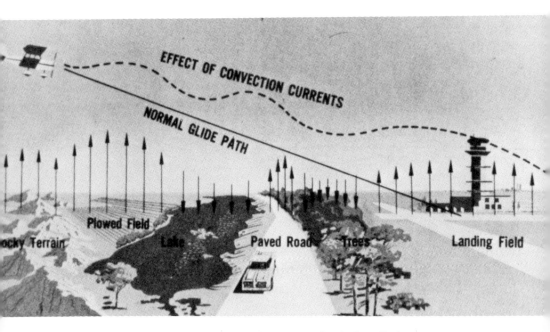

Up and down air currents affect any ultralight's flight.

ing thermal, using it to gain altitude. You often find rising warm air over factories, or big paved parking lots, or radiating from rocky hills. This, too, may mean thermals. Often a flying ultralighter will switch off the engine and ride the thermals in the same style as a sailplaner or hang glider.

On the other hand, rather than radiating heat, cold areas draw air toward them, causing downdrafts. A lake, a green field, or a patch of snow tends to pull air toward it. As an ultralighter you should learn to read the signs and thereby be prepared to adjust your controls to sudden up and down surges of the aircraft as it finds itself in the grip of changing currents.

The air movement to be most concerned about, however, is the wind. Winds are more sudden, and often more forceful, than currents. A strong wind of over twelve knots usually is a major nemesis to an ultralight pilot. The planes are too low powered and lightweight to give battle to this.

You must learn to read the signs of wind. Smoke from a chimney, ripples moving across a lake, dust behind a moving car, the bending of treetops are a few ways of telling both the velocity and the direction of a wind. You must read the signs to avoid getting into strong wind conditions.

In addition to visual signs, radio forecasts or local newspaper weather reports are helpful in providing a general idea of what you can expect in terms of weather.

Also you should know that winds are deflected upward on windward sides of hills, while a downdraft probably exists on the leeward side. Any objects such as barns, buildings, or tall trees disrupt the smooth flow of a wind, causing a turbulence that you must take into account during takeoff and landing.

All part of meteorology, the many activities of the atmosphere should be part of your basic knowledge. It is far preferable to learn beforehand than to be caught unprepared later on when cruising around high above the ground.

Navigation, perhaps, is one of the less necessary skills for ultralighting. Flying the short-range aircraft, you usually will get around by using simple pilotage. Flying in clear and calm weather—the safest way to travel—you keep your course in view. You fly from one visual landmark or checkpoint to the next. You really have little need for sophisticated navigational instruments or procedures.

However, with experience you may want to take longer flights, perhaps stretch out into cross-country excursions. In that case you should at least carry a compass and know how to read it. Also before taking long flights you must

Ultralighters can usually get around by using pilotage.

acquaint yourself with the use of government printed aeronautical sectional charts issued for different regions of the country. Sometimes these are called "sectionals." They are detailed ground maps providing flying data not found elsewhere. They show the location of emergency airstrips, prominent landmarks, and the types of obstructions along the way. They also show military installations and other types of retricted areas that you must stay clear of. To be a skillful flyer, it is important to know how to use sectional charts because, complicated though they may seem, they are designed specifically to help you navigate and make proper use of the airspace.

On the whole, by the time you have a good amount of ground school study behind you, you have a different view of flying and a pretty fair idea of what to look for once you are introduced to your ultralight aircraft.

You can hardly wait.

# 4. GETTING READY

It is barely dawn, and chilly, when you arrive at the open field where you will help assemble the ultralight aircraft in which you will learn to fly.

There is a good reason for the early start. The calm hours of the day are best for flying the miniweight airplanes. This is around dawn or dusk, when windless conditions often exist. One FAA ruling is that an ultralight can be flown only between sunrise and sunset. However, if the plane is equipped with operating warning lights, you are allowed to stretch the flight time from a half hour before official sunrise to a half hour beyond sunset, when the sights from the air are often most interesting and colorful.

This morning you find that several other ultralight enthusiasts have arrived before you. By the light of a car's headlamps, one ultralighter and his teenage son and daughter are carefully removing a homebuilt plane from a trailer. The family has carefully constructed the entire air-

A pair of dedicated ultralighters get an early start on the day.

craft from detailed plans. They had purchased the plans and basic building instructions for less than a hundred dollars from an aircraft engineer who had made and successfully flown several of his own models. The whole plane, including the engine, had cost them a little more than $2,000.

"But it took us four months of working evenings and weekends," the builder tells you. "We had to shop all over for materials, and then cut, shape, and bend each part to fit the plans. Tubing, wood, and fabric. It was a big job. Next time I would be tempted to pay the extra money and buy a precut kit." Yet, you can easily tell that the whole family is proud of their handiwork. Since no official inspection is demanded of an ultralight, it behooves the builders to be sure that the craft is safe and airworthy before attempting to lift it off the ground. So they will proceed slowly, step by small step, and check everything out thoroughly.

Shortly four young people arrive with a plane that they had made from a precut and presewn kit. All they had had to do was follow the charts, line up the holes, and put the machine together. It had a strong double-surfaced wing built of spars and ribs and covered with strong rip-proof Dacron. The ultralight was of the king post and cable braced design. The long wing came apart at the center so the two halves folded like an umbrella, ready to be stored in a special trailer alongside the fuselage for easy transportation. The kit cost about twice what the family who worked from plans and raw material had paid.

Quite a few ultralights fold into trailer-sized packages.

Just as the first orange rays of a rising sun begin to stain the horizon, the fellow for whom you are waiting arrives. He's a young Certified Flight Instructor (CFI), properly licensed to teach you to fly. Laid along the top of his compact car, snubbed down with several bungee cords, is a long blue bundle about a dozen feet long. Straddling it is the landing gear assembly, a sort of three-wheeled cage of bent aluminum tubing.

Although they call this one "ready to fly," it obviously will take a little putting together before it is truly an aircraft. For the sake of cartop portability it was disassembled after its last flight. Complete with engine, which is tucked in the car trunk, this plane costs in the neighborhood of $5,000. You have heard that it can be assembled and made ready to fly in about a half hour.

The most portable ultralights can be car-topped.

You hurry over to greet your instructor. Already he has guided you carefully through the early stages of ground school. Some instructors prefer to give flying training first, then bring in the ground school phase. They feel that once you have learned basic flying and know what to look for, the subjects of aerodynamics, meteorology, and navigation fit into place and are more easily understood. It is really a matter of individual preference.

You have found your instructor both knowledgeable and patient. He is the dealer for a particular brand of ultralight. In fact, most ultralight instructors are involved in flying or selling a specific aircraft. So their courses of instruction, while basic to all flying, are also tailored to the type of ultralight with which they deal.

A course of instruction is usually required with the purchase of a plane, but it is not included in the price. No reputable dealer will let a buyer tote his or her new ultralight out to some field, attach the wings, and learn to fly it by trial-and-error methods. Proper instruction is strongly recommended. Even experienced pilots of airliners or private planes need additional training in order to fly an ultralight safely. The miniaircraft have flying characteristics that are often quite different from those of larger, more powerful airplanes.

A student learns early to rely on the instructor.

It is not necessary to buy an ultralight in order to learn to fly one. Some people prefer to see how well they like this kind of flying before joining a flying club or considering the purchase of a craft, and learning to fly one is about the only sure way to find out. Whether separate, or with the purchase of a plane, a course of instruction is available to anyone who wants to take it. The course may stretch over two or three weekends, include both preflight and flying training, and cost from around $300 to perhaps

$500. Any dealer or ultralight flyer can tell you where proper instructions can be obtained.

In your case, you have chosen to see how well you take to the art of flying before going more deeply into the expense of buying or sharing the cost of an ultralight, so you have signed up for instructions. Even if you discover that you relish flying and breeze through the course, you still may find it to your advantage to rent an ultralight whenever you want to take to the sky. At least for a while. Dealers often rent ultralights to qualified pilots at prices as low as $25 an hour.

Now you pitch in and help your instructor lift the wrapped-up aircraft from his cartop. You find a clean patch of ground and lay down the long zippered bag containing all of the dismantled airplane except the landing gear and engine.

Each ultralight has a proper order of assembly that must be carefully followed while getting it ready for the air. Once removed from the trailer, some just need to have their wings and empennage unfolded and the components securely locked into place with assorted types of nuts, bolts, and so-called safe pins or "safeties," and they are virtually ready to fly. There is little need for wrenches or screwdrivers. In their proper places, safeties keep nuts,

Key-ringlike safeties secure critical parts of an ultralight in place.

bolts, tubing or rivets from slipping out or loosening.

Some ultralights, like the Eagle that you are about to help assemble, come with everything precut, bent, sewn, and drilled. You need only familiarize yourself with the owner's manual to learn the proper sequence of putting the parts together. Above all, you must know how to adjust, tighten, and secure them into a safe and airworthy position.

You help your instructor unzip the long nylon carrying case. Inside you see what looks like a random pile of aluminum tubing, steel-wire cables, and folded Dacron, topped off by a loose wooden propeller, the only item that even hints of the jumble of parts ending up as an aircraft.

As you unfold the wing and spread it out on the ground, its brightly patterned Dacron gives it the appearance of a giant butterfly sunning itself on the cool soil. You move along the limp trailing edge of the wing and slip lengths of bent aluminum tubing into special pockets sewn into the fabric. Very much the way battens are slipped into a boat's sail, these ribs stiffen the wing and give it its aerodynamic shape.

Plane parts are laid out carefully before assembly begins.

You further brace the wing by raising the vertical king
post above the wing center. The king post supports the
series of stainless steel cables that reach out to various
points of the main wing and to the small canard wing located out on the sturdy length of aluminum tubing that
serves as the Eagle's spine or keel. Like a ship's bowsprit, it
thrusts out forward of the wing.

Other cables stretch taut from beneath the wing to focal
points on the fuselage, which is really nothing more than
a cage of small tubing that forms the three-wheeled landing gear and contains the harness seat and flight controls.
Thus, the strong cables brace the plane against pressures
and strains from any direction.

King post and steel cables strengthen an ultralight and make it
airworthy.

Instead of a tail rudder, the Eagle, like several other designs of ultralights, has small drag rudders on each wingtip. The wingtip rudders operate in much the same manner as normal rudders, deflecting air and causing the plane to initiate a turn.

With rudders in place, you help the instructor hang the seat inside the cockpit located between the wing and the wheels. The seat is like a swing, hanging from the aircraft's overhead keel. Several thin cables connect to it, and to a bicycle-handlebar-type control yoke directly in front of the seat. A shift of weight or pressure on the yoke moves the control surfaces that guide the plane. The seat has a safety harness to prevent you from slipping or falling out.

With the canard attached, the wing in place, and the cockpit rigged, the airframe is fully assembled. You double-check everything.

The instructor opens up the back of his car and lifts out the power pack. It is a small single-cylinder two-cycle engine. It has a short propeller shaft protruding rearward from a nest of belts and pulleys that reduce the fast engine rpm's to a slower and more efficient propeller speed.

You hold the engine up while the instructor bolts it to the aircraft's keel, above and behind the cockpit. Then he slips the small wedge-shaped plastic gas tank into a pocket above the engine and hooks up the fuel line.

The lightweight two-cycle engine is put in place.

The last item to go into place is the propeller, a brightly varnished, laminated wood thruster.

Again you follow your teacher as he gives the craft a preflight safety inspection. He jiggles the braces, checks the bolts, fasteners, and lock pins for secure placement. Then, of all things, he reaches up, takes hold of the plane's keel tube, and gives the whole aircraft a vigorous shake. Nothing falls off or seems to creak or rattle unduly. He turns to you and smiles.

"Okay," he says, "let's see if it will fly."

# 5. FLIGHT TRAINING

You feel that you have done well during the preflight ground schooling and have also learned the fundamentals for assembling an ultralight. You are delighted to at last be getting into the actual flying training.

But you know that your instructor will be watching you closely. He has told you from the beginning that he will move you step by step just as fast, but no faster, than is comfortable for you. He can tell by how smoothly you progress.

Each of the many different brands of ultralights is assembled and flown in a different way. However, regardless of the aircraft being used, flight training generally follows a standard procedure and progresses in well laid-out steps. After you have learned to fly one ultralight—really learned the basics of aerodynamics and control—you should have little difficulty adapting to another type later. In fact, training in ultralights has proved to be a good step toward

becoming a licensed pilot, if you are moving in that direction.

Different instructors also use different methods and
equipment for flight training. A few use a simulator. This
may be a sort of engineless dummy ultralight mounted on
a framework hung out in front of a truck or other moving
vehicle. The simulator is hinged, or gimballed, enabling
the aircraft to tilt in the three attitudes of flight—yaw,
pitch, and roll.

As the vehicle on which the simulator is mounted accelerates at a carefully regulated speed, it generates wind
over the wing, producing lift. With the instructor close at
hand to talk the student through each step, the student in
the simulator works the controls to put the craft through
the motions of flying.

However, simulators are not commonly available. Most
instructors have their own flight training systems. Frequently, after the instructor is satisfied that the student has
mastered the ground courses, he will turn the novice pilot
loose in the airplane. This is not really that foolhardy, for,
although the student may seem to be going it alone during
taxi runs and while bunny-hopping the plane along an airstrip, the instructor is always near at hand directing him or
her carefully every step of the way by walkie-talkie. No

Having learned proper basics, a supervised student may go bunny-hopping to get the feel of flying.

qualified instructor will allow a student to spread his or her wings before that person is ready to fly.

Your own flight training in the Eagle, with which you are now fairly familiar, begins early one morning on a small, private airstrip that the owner allows ultralighters to use for practice. With the plane assembled and checked out, you position it at the end of the runway. As though he wants to be sure that you have done your homework properly, the instructor leads you around the aircraft. He points to various functioning parts such as the control cables, steering yoke, throttle, rudders, and elevator and asks you to explain to him what they do and how they function. Having paid close attention during the several ses-

Ground test all controls such as rudder pedals, if any.

sions of ground training, and having digested the aircraft
owner's manual that has been provided, you are ready
with the answers. You review what you have learned.

Seeming satisfied, your instructor motions for you to
strap yourself into the seat. He hands you a small CB
walkie-talkie unit and helps you plug in the earphone.

"You won't need a microphone," he says. "I'll do the
talking; you do the listening." He taps the engine "kill
switch" mounted on the airframe beside you. "Use that
switch whenever you want to shut down the power. If anything unexpected happens during your taxi tests, hit it."

You pull on your helmet. Then, as you have been
trained to do, you look about to be sure there is no one
near the propeller.

"Prop clear!" you call the warning anyway.

You reach up and give the starter cord a yank. Then another. On the third pull the cold engine comes alive. You back off on the motorcycle-type throttle at the right tip of the steering yoke to keep the ultralight from starting to move before you want it to.

Most ultralight engines are started with a pull cord.

"Ease into it," your instructor says, after checking the walkie-talkie to be sure you hear him above the engine sound. Then he moves away and climbs into the back of the small car he is using to lead you through your taxi tests. "Just follow directions," he adds. "Okay, give her a little more power. Let's see how straight you can taxi down the centerline."

You rotate the throttle a bit. The engine revs up and the pusher propeller behind you gets louder. The ultralight slowly begins to move. You sight down the white centerline of the paved runway, and try to hold the nosewheel on it. You are going too slowly for the aerodynamic controls to take affect, so you steer by using the nosewheel footbar.

Practice taxiing.

"Very good," your instructor's voice comes through your earphone. "Now try a few S-turns. And give yourself a bit more throttle."

Still using nosewheel steering, you swing the aircraft back and forth across the centerline in a series of lazy S-turns. Moving a bit faster, but far below the twenty mph takeoff speed, the plane becomes more sensitive to the mildly gusting breeze. It's nothing to be concerned about at the moment. You concentrate primarily on adjusting the throttle to control engine power. The more throttle you use to increase the velocity of the airstream brushing the wing and control surfaces, the more the little plane seems to perk up and come alive. She hardens, as they say.

All in all, after about an hour of repeated taxiing up and down the runway, needing fewer and fewer instructions over the radio, you feel that you have gained mastery over the ultralight, at least while taxiing at relatively low speed.

Still directing you from under the open hatchback of the pace car, your instructor allows you to increase your speed in well-regulated steps. At what you guess to be about ten miles per hour, the rudders become effective, and you no longer need to steer by the nosewheel. Now, with more power, a stronger wind in your face, and the use of aerodynamic controls, you begin to get the feel of flying, although your wheels are still firmly on the ground. A couple times your momentum builds up too fast, your nosewheel starts to come up off the ground, and your instructor cautions you to ease back on the throttle.

You practice a few S-turns at the higher taxi speed, throttling back and turning downwind to recover balance whenever an unseen gust tilts a wingtip toward the ground.

Phasing from slow to fast taxi goes nicely. You have been told that towing comes next. This means that you

The instructor conducts taxi tests from the rear of a pace vehicle.

will soon be deliberately lifting the wheels off the ground. You feel that you are ready, but first you take a little break to think over what you have done so far.

Then, before you get back in the plane, the instructor leads you through a repeat of the preflight checks. You look particularly for loose bolts and fasteners, and tangled cables. You don't bother to start the engine, for it won't be used during the tow training.

Your instructor attaches a special towing bridle to the front of the Eagle. He then stretches a long yellow nylon rope between the bridle and the tow vehicle. He tells you that the driver will regulate the speed of the car, and that all you have to do is to operate the plane controls.

"Let's take it slowly step by step," he repeats his basic philosophy of training. "And don't worry. If anything goes wrong I can release the tow rope and you will simply coast to a stop." To give you an idea of what he wants, your instructor slips into the seat and buckles up. As you watch from the rear of the tow car, he demonstrates how towing maneuvers are done.

When he is finished, you change places with him, check your harness and radio, and wait for the tow vehicle to start moving. With the engine off, all is quiet. The tow car picks up speed, increasing the whistle of the wind

Buckling in for the towing tests.

through the wire braces. The airspeed indicator is with the tow car driver to help her regulate the speed, so you are not sure how fast you are going. But when you guess your speed to be between fifteen and eighteen miles per hour, you feel a definite firmness in the control bar as the stiffening windstream presses against the plane.

At the instructor's direction you push against the nosewheel crossbar with your feet. This shifts your weight rearward of the aircraft's center of gravity, or balancing point, and the elevator aft of the canard wing tilts downward. Your nosewheel lifts a few inches off the ground. You shift your weight forward again to bring it down. (Instead of weight-shifting, many solid-seat ultralights having three-axis control systems use a joystick to activate elevators to pitch the aircraft up or down, just as do most small private aircraft.)

You rather enjoy the coordinated combination of weight-shifting and aerodynamic controls that the Eagle uses. It adds to the sensation that you are really flying the birdlike machine. You repeat the lifting and lowering of the nosewheel a few times, relishing your body control over the plane.

"How are you doing?" your instructor asks over the radio.

"Great!" you reply enthusiastically, hoping he shares your high opinion.

"Let's do a little flying," he says. "Stay centered on the runway and just do as I say."

Starting from the very end of the runway, the tow car picks up speed.

"Ease back."

Again, as you have done before, you push with your feet, swinging your seat harness slightly rearward. Again the shift of weight causes the nosewheel to come up, more quickly this time.

"Hold her there."

Balanced on the two main wheels, with the nosewheel up off the ground, you taxi down the runway at a crisp clip.

"Okay. Off you go."

You feel the increasing speed of the wind in your face, and see the gently curving tow rope straighten a bit due to the additional drag on the aircraft. Then, almost without your knowing it, the main wheels come off the ground.

You're flying! Being towed, but flying. Climbing.

Being towed into the air provides the first real feel of flying.

"Ease forward," the voice cautions in your ear. "Bring her level."

You shift your weight just slightly forward in the sling seat, and the nose comes down. You neutralize your position, level off, and hold it there, skimming along about five feet off the runway. There is no comment over the radio, but you know that your instructor has to be pleased. You sure are.

Then, approaching the end of the runway, the tow car slowly decreases speed. You just sit and the aircraft settles gently to the ground and rolls to a stop. You don't even try to hide your grin.

While you are being ground-towed slowly back to the downwind end of the runway, your instructor debriefs you over the radio. In essence, you are doing fine, but don't get overconfident. Especially, don't get cocky. Maybe he was concerned about that big grin you had flashed moments earlier.

Now, in position, the tow car accelerates from the end of the runway. Picking up speed quickly, you feel almost like an old hand at the controls as you lift off and settle into level flight.

"Take her higher."

You shift your weight slightly back and watch the ca-

Engine-off towing enables the student to master the controls.

nard tilt skyward. Up. Up. With slight alarm you look along the yellow rope angling sharply downward to the tow vehicle. The hatchback coupe has shrunk to the size of a toy model, and you can hardly see the upturned face of the instructor.

"Good. You're at twenty feet."

Twenty feet? You feel as though you're a mile high.

"Try some gentle turns. Now, don't over-control."

You put a little steering pressure on the control yoke.

The aircraft responds and turns gently. You center the control, move it back in the opposite direction, and swing back across the centerline and to the opposite side of the runway. You note that one wingtip is slightly lower than the other and believe that you are gently banking your turns, just as it should be done.

The towed flights continue for a while. Your confidence increases, but you are careful not to let it over-build, particularly after the caution from your instructor.

"Ready for some landings?"

"I—I guess so."

"You guess so?"

"I'm ready."

So you start another run. After towing you back to altitude, your instructor drops his end of the tow rope. Although still attached at your end, you quickly overrun its dangling length and watch it disappear below and behind the plane. Dragging on the ground, it causes no problem.

You are gliding free. In order to maintain proper flying speed, you put your weight forward, lowering the nose. The ground comes up a little too fast, and you correct by shifting your weight slightly rearward.

When you're a scant two feet off the ground, you shove back still more. The nose comes up to a rather steep angle. In flaring out, the plane decelerates. As it loses flying speed, it settles to the ground with a gentle thump. You let it roll a few yards, then apply the nosewheel brake.

"I've seen worse . . ." your instructor acknowledges as you start to unbuckle. You wonder if he is going to finish the sentence with some kind of stinging criticism. Actually, you think you did quite well—that is, without being cocky, you think so.

Then he smiles and puts his hand on your shoulder. "Want to try it again?"

"Yes, sir," you reply. "And again and again!"

Whether he thinks you are being cocky or not, you simply cannot control your grin and sense of accomplishment.

# 6. SAFETY FIRST

As the time approaches when you will start wheeling freely around in the sky like an unfettered bird, you need to step back and take a good look at what you will face as a pilot.

"If man were meant to fly, he would have been born with wings." It's a wheezy old saying you've heard a dozen times, but it contains an implied warning that should not be ignored. To fly is to accept risk. How well you are prepared to handle the risks may determine how long you stay healthy and happy.

In order to lessen the undeniable dangers of flying, you must pay close attention to various safety factors. Three major areas of safety are personal safety, safety of your aircraft, and the rules and regulations to be followed in the interest of overall flying safety.

At all times your personal safety depends largely on how well you have mastered your lessons during the training period. You have learned from books, demonstrations, and early experiences with the aircraft.

The first rule of safety is to be sure the aircraft is properly assembled to fly.

You add to personal safety, as well as to comfort, by dressing properly for open-air flying. Always remembering that the higher you go the colder it gets, you should wear ample, windproof-type clothing. It should be reasonably close-fitting. Loose, floppy clothing whipping in the wind is both distracting and uncomfortable. A good wind-breaker, preferably insulated, is needed for most early morning and evening flying.

Your shoes should also be resistant to cold, and fairly soft soled so they won't slip on the rudder controls or foot

Proper dress is important to both safety and comfort.

rests. Heavy ski socks add welcome protection when flying under cold conditions. Gloves are a handy addition.

A good helmet is your most vital protection. Generally helmets are made in layers of built-up fiberglass cloth or of a stress resistant and impact-tested plastic compound. Some helmets are open-faced, in which case you need some kind of a face plate or goggles to protect you from the windstream. Others provide full head and face protection.

Importantly, you should choose a helmet that has a

DOT (Department of Transportation) certification sticker on it. Such government-tested helmets are favored by motorcyclists, snowmobilers, and other advocates of fast-action sports.

Fit your helmet carefully. It should be snug but not too tight. Put it on and tighten the chinstrap to normal tension. Stiffen your neck, grasp the sides of the helmet, and rock it forward and back, and side to side. For lasting comfort and best protection it should move a few degrees, but no more. You might want to add a snap-on visor to combat the sun's glare.

Since your helmet is your best insurance, you certainly should shop carefully and not compromise on quality. Beware of trade-in helmets or those you see around swap meets. Most helmet materials become brittle with age, or

The helmet is the most important item of dress.

deteriorate under the onslaught of fuel chemicals, exhaust fumes, and impurities ever-present in the atmosphere.

For major emergencies two types of parachutes are available to ultralighters. One is a normal chest-pack that can be used when a pilot has to bail out and leave the aircraft to its destruction. The other is a ballistic recovery system that attaches to the airplane itself. When triggered, an explosive device deploys the large parachute that lowers both the pilot and the ultralight safely, though not particularly gently, to the ground.

You must carefully watch how you operate an ultra-

Chest-pack personal parachutes are frequently worn.

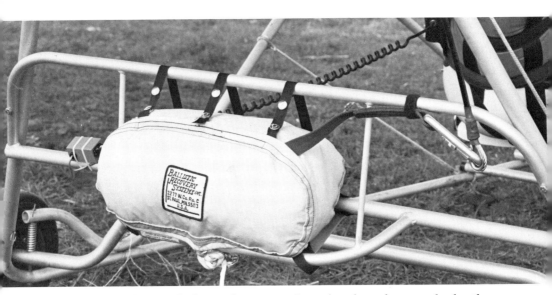

This tightly packed parachute is explosively released to save both pilot and ultralight plane.

light. You should never attempt to make it do what it was not designed for. By FAA regulation an ultralight's speed must be kept below 55 knots, or 63 mph. By putting strain on the engine, particularly during a shallow dive, you can make most ultralights exceed the speed limit. But you do it at the risk of shedding a wing or causing other structural failure. Optimum cruising speeds vary with different ultralights, with 35–45 mph being a fair average. So heed your airspeed indicator, and keep safely under the so-called Vne, or never-exceed velocity.

Also use your altimeter to be aware of how high or low you are flying. Judgment of height is difficult, especially when flying over water or hills, and you may be deceived into believing you are higher than you are—a dangerous situation to be in. The altimeter takes away the guesswork.

In a relatively slow-moving ultralight, you may not feel the elevatorlike sensations of gaining or losing vertical altitude quickly that may occur in a thermal or sudden downdraft. A variometer, or rate-of-climb indicator, keeps you well informed of sudden altitude variations. It enables you to make immediate corrections and avoid possible mishaps or, indeed, crashes.

A few basic flight and engine instruments add much to the safety factor.

Long before ultralights became popular, the Federal Aviation Administration established safety guidelines to be followed by all aircraft. Although the FAA has allowed ultralight pilots the freedom of self-regulation, ultralighters still must observe the basic FAA rules of safety. These are spelled out in what is called Part 91 of the Federal Air Regulations (FAR). In late 1982 an additional Part 103 that applies more specifically to ultralights was issued. All ultralight flyers must adhere to the operating requirements included in FAR Parts 91 and 103.

Although a wise pilot need not be reminded, the FAA insists that you check over, or preflight, your plane before every flight. If you intend to leave the local vicinity from where you take off and go on a cross-country jaunt, you must check the weather. This is best done by calling the nearest Flight Service Station (FSS) for the latest weather report along your intended route. The FSS is listed in your phone book under U.S. Government.

You shouldn't need reminding, but the FAA insists that you buckle your seat belt or harness any time you are in the aircraft, whether on the ground or in the air. Helmet, too, of course.

FAR Part 91 prohibits any reckless or careless operation of the aircraft. Sometimes this is not easy to define. Yet, should you buzz a ball park or attempt some stunts over a

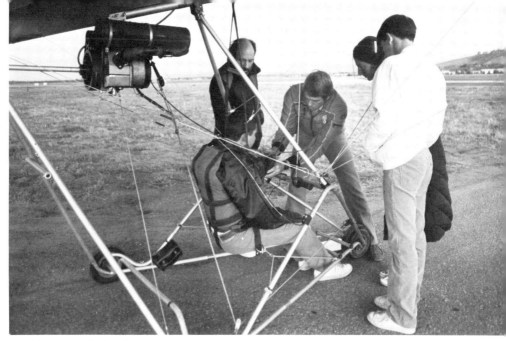

Buckle up and check it out.

crowd, you can be pretty sure of hearing from the FAA, and you will likely be fined.

Dropping anything from your aircraft that could possibly hurt someone or damage property is prohibited. Even if you drop something as harmless as leaflets, you may be cited by local authorities for littering.

Since no ultralight is equipped with sophisticated navigational instruments needed for blind flying, you must operate only in Visual Flight Rule (VFR) conditions during daylight hours. Generally that means you need three miles of horizontal visibility. You must not venture too close to clouds, and certainly not enter one. Stay at least 500 feet beneath clouds if you are flying low, and don't get closer

When flying an ultralight, it's best to keep well away from all clouds.

than 1,000 feet to the cloud tops if you are at high altitude. If you should venture foolishly into a cloud, the turbulence can tear your plane apart, or, in the dark gray mass you may become disoriented. Your sense of balance goes haywire and you will likely lose control of your aircraft. You could even collide with some other witless and reckless pilot. Clouds are part of weather, and weather is not to be challenged in an ultralight.

FAR Part 103 prohibits flight over congested areas, except with special permission, since you may have no safe place to make an emergency landing without endangering people or property. If you find yourself having to cross over such an area, stay at least 1,000 feet over the tallest structures. Should anything go wrong, this altitude provides you with approximately 1½ miles of gliding distance in which to locate a suitable landing spot. Always keep some landing spot in sight just in case of such an emergency.

It is wise to fly below 3,000 feet and stay clear of any area where there is apt to be air traffic of other heavier and faster planes. Stay away from airports that have operating towers. Since it's unlikely that you have a two-way radio, you have no way of keeping in touch with the tower, nor of knowing when you may be wandering into an air traffic pattern. Ultralights are not intended to share airspace with commercial aviation. Your plane is a recreational vehicle, meant to be flown well away from other aviation activity.

There is nothing wrong with using private airstrips, however, as long as you have the owner's permission and abide by whatever rules he or she may have regarding traffic patterns, parking, and such. This applies, of course, to your use of any private property. Unless it's an emergency situation, you don't land in some farmer's pasture at the risk of spooking his cows or plowing into a strawberry patch.

Small, private, isolated airfields are favored by ultralighters.

You must always be considerate of others, which will pay off in much-needed goodwill and cooperation. Not all groundlings share your enthusiasm for ultralighting. They may get downright hostile if you swoop around early in the morning waking them from a sound sleep, or scattering their chickens with your giant hawklike shadow.

At times you may be sharing airspace with other vehicles. Being lightweight and low-powered, you usually fly low and slow. This makes your craft, next to a hang glider and a hot-air balloon, the most vulnerable object in the sky. Even birds have no trouble outmaneuvering you. But generally if you keep looking around to "clear the sky," you can find plenty of safe flying space.

You must avoid flying over military installations, flight training and testing centers, and any other restricted zones marked out on your sectional chart. Actually you won't be

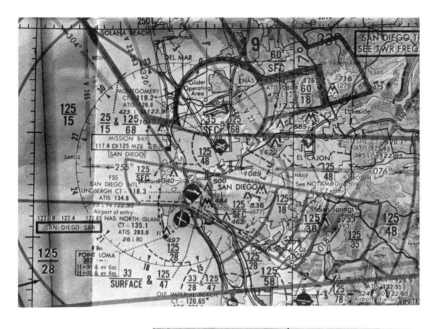

Sectional charts provide important data (above), as well as important words and signs of precaution for far-ranging flyers (right).

concerned with such limitations unless you live and fly near one or plan to make some long-distance flights across unfamiliar areas.

When you share the sky with other man-made flying objects you must know and abide by certain rules of the road. Being so slow and vulnerable, you should always be on the defensive. In contrast to nautical tradition, where a powerboat gives way to a sailboat, your flimsy craft does not have the right-of-way over a Twin Cessna descending toward a distant airport. The highly maneuverable Cessna probably will turn aside, but don't depend on it. Give way. Better still, don't be flying in areas where Cessnas are apt to appear.

Any aircraft in distress, however, has right-of-way over other aircraft. And when two aircraft converge, the one on the right has the right-of-way. But don't insist on it. Clear out of the way.

When two aircraft approach head on both should veer right and pass well clear of each other.

During a landing, the aircraft that is lowest on the final approach has the right-of-way. Yet, again, you must give way immediately to any aircraft in obvious trouble.

Most rules of safety are based on common sense. As a pilot, you will know when you are overreaching the capabilities of your plane and yourself. If you stretch things too far you are bound to get into trouble sooner or later.

So, know your aircraft. Study the owner's manual, and, above all, remember what it says. The manual will detail how to check and service different parts, and when it is wise to replace them. Neither manufacturer nor instructor will do anything to encourage you to take risks. Quite the contrary. Although some ultralights are capable of being looped, rolled, or spun, to attempt such maneuvers is foolhardy, irresponsible, and dangerous.

So, all in all, know and abide by the rules of safety, both the printed formal ones and those that are based on simple common sense, for only in safety can you find the real joys of ultralight flying. Always abide by the timeworn but true motto:

Safety first, last, and always!

# 7. SOLO PILOT

Although your instructor hasn't said anything, you feel that this is the day when you will get to take the ultralight up alone. You have learned a lot during the past sessions, both during ground training and out on the flying field. You feel ready—and confident.

By the time you have the ultralight assembled, the sun is just clearing the eastern foothills. This time your instructor has done more watching than helping. He insists that your ability to assemble and disassemble the aircraft is almost as important as your being able to fly it. "Leave out a bolt, or forget to secure a connection," he warns, "and your flying career could be a short one."

He starts you out with a few more runs at the end of the tow rope. You practice takeoffs and landings and add some gently banked turns thirty feet off the ground. A couple of the landings are a bit rough. But the others are smooth enough to bring moderate praise over the two-way radio.

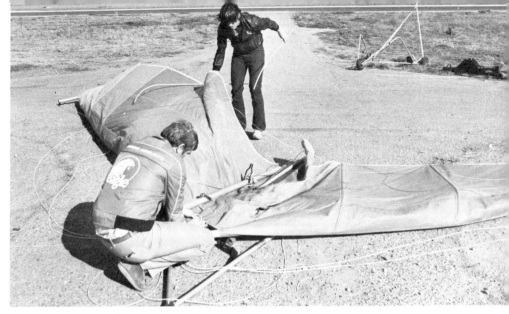

Aircraft assembly is the first order of the day.

At the end of the session you still feel pepped up and ready to go, free of the mental and physical exhaustion you had experienced during earlier lessons.

Returning to the parking apron, you unbuckle and climb out of the seat. You wait for the usual debriefing, hoping that the rougher of the landings weren't too noticeable. Your instructor is looking closely at you. You return his gaze.

"Not bad," he says, smiling faintly. "You want to light her up again and see how she flies—without a rope?"

"Yes, sir!" you say without hesitation.

"Okay, how do you start?"

There is no doubt in your mind. He has drummed into

you that every flight starts with a thorough walkaround preflight inspection of the aircraft. Always. Without a word, you set about doing it. You begin at the nose and work slowly to your right, counterclockwise around the plane.

Following a checklist, you inspect all nuts and bolts, making sure that they are secure and safetied. You feel the

Careful preflight inspection precedes every flight.

cables for proper tension and search for any frayed or broken strands. As you progress around the aircraft looking for dents or cracks in the tubing, you carefully scan the fabric for wrinkles or tears.

You continue on around the aircraft, looking over the propeller for nicks or cracks. You check the tires and axles of the landing gear. You inspect the engine bolts, the fuel line connections, and assure yourself that there is a full tank. You see that the instruments are in order. You move the controls and work the throttle to be sure it doesn't bind. You check the seat harness and belts.

After completing the circle and inspecting every part, large and small, you back away a few yards to get an overall view of the aircraft.

"How does she look?" your instructor asks.

"I believe she's airworthy," you reply.

"You believe?"

"She's ready to fly," you amend. You should know your instructor doesn't welcome any signs of uncertainty.

He smiles. "Good job. You didn't miss a thing. In fact, I'm willing to try it myself. You stay down here and watch."

As he has done before, your instructor operates the controls, starts the engine, and takes off. You keep a mental

The instructor often takes the first flight to check everything out.

log of the pattern he flies and will expect you to follow on your first flight. His flight lasts about ten minutes.

Back on the ground he kills the engine and climbs out.

"Got it?" he asks.

"Yep."

"Okay, she's all yours."

Trying to hide your excitement, you settle into the seat and buckle up. After setting the carburetor choke, you look around to be sure it's safe to start up, and call, "Clear prop!"

You give the starter cord several easy pulls to prime the carburetor. Then you give a hefty yank on the T-handle. The engine coughs but doesn't start. Another sharp yank. The engine catches, spinning the prop. You check around

Settling into the cockpit on your first solo flight.

once more to be sure no one is in the danger area near the quite invisibly spinning prop. You throttle back to a decent warm-up idle.

On your own power, you taxi out to the end of the runway. Your instructor stands at the edge of the field, walkie-talkie in hand.

"Start with a few touch-and-go landings." His voice comes into your headset. "Don't get more than a couple yards off the ground. Use mostly throttle. Add throttle when you want to rise, cut back if you want to descend. Understand?"

"Got it," you nod.

As you open the throttle, the little plane quickly picks up speed. You open the throttle wider. The nosewheel comes up and the mains lift off at a speed of a little over

Takeoff.

twenty miles per hour. Suddenly you are cruising a couple yards off the ground. You hold the plane level for about fifty yards, then ease back on the throttle and settle on the ground with a gentle thump.

"Not bad," the voice gives you guarded praise. "Try a few more."

You do it again. Over and over. Touch-and-go. With each landing and takeoff you gain confidence.

Then the instructions are to go a little higher and try a few gentle S-turns. You perform them smoothly, just as you had during the towing training. You hardly realize that you are fully controlling the plane.

Except for one rather hard landing, you know you have

been doing a good job at the controls. At least, you feel so. After a half dozen or so up-and-down flights along the runway, your instructor tells you to return to the parking ramp.

"How do you feel?"

"Great." You grin again.

"How's the fuel?"

You look at the transparent plastic tank, about three-fourths full of the tan-colored oil-and-gas mixture. "Plenty of fuel," you say, half-suspecting and fully hoping what may be about to happen.

"Okay. What are you hanging around here for? Take her up. But stay in sight. Do what you want for about ten minutes. Then fly a proper pattern, make a decent landing, and we'll consider that you are . . . uh . . . on your way to becoming a pilot."

You preflight the plane once more, then taxi back to the far end of the runway. Although your ultralight will take off in less than a hundred feet, there is real comfort in having a whole long runway out ahead to land on in case something goes wrong.

Facing into the gentle breeze, you blip the throttle a couple of times to clear the engine's throat. You glory in the feel of being totally alone—just you and the mini-airplane nestling you under its spreading wing.

Solo. You are about to embark upon your first real solo flight. A cherished reward for your hours of studying and training.

You make a final engine check. Then you go through the controls and watch the different surfaces move and adjust to your touch. You pull down the faceplate of your helmet, take a deep breath, and twist the throttle open.

The tiny engine roars. The propeller is a spinning blur behind you. As though released from a slingshot, the ultralight leaps forward. You hold it to the ground for a dozen yards while it builds up momentum. Then you push back with your body to unweight the front end. The nosewheel lifts just before the mains, and the lightweight aircraft leaps skyward. You hold it in the climb for a

Taking off steeply into the wind.

while, then start steering left and away from the runway. You glance at the altimeter. At about four hundred feet you level off. Looking down, you are amazed at how quickly everything has shrunken in size.

You retard the throttle to cruising speed. You sigh and settle comfortably in your hanging seat, trying to control the excitement surging through you. As you were trained to do, you survey the ground and keep a potential landing spot in sight. You flip up your protective faceplate and let the thirty-five mile an hour windstream buffet your cheeks. It's cold, invigorating, thrilling. When it gets a little too cold and peppery you close your helmet again.

You are happily amazed at how naturally you move the controls in order to smooth out unsuspected air currents that rock the plane. In fact, without even realizing it, you find that your equilibrium is constantly adjusting automatically to every movement of the plane. Although you churn with excitement, you feel strangely at home in the sky.

From aloft the earth becomes an entirely different planet. Peaceful and brightly colored, it has turned into a patchwork quilt of fields, houses, streams, and roads.

You cruise around glorying in the scenery and the feeling of freedom. Your radio remains silent, so you figure that you are not doing anything too badly or you would be hearing from your instructor.

Long before you want to, you realize that you have used up your ten minutes of birdlike action high in the sky. Just for good measure, you swing around in a couple of nicely banked turns. You practice some semi-stalls and recoveries: You lift the nose and throttle back until the plane loses flying speed and begins to flutter. But you quickly drop the nose and add power to pull out of it. It is no real problem, particularly in the canard-equipped Eagle that all but eliminates the danger of the craft stalling. Being out front, if the small canard loses its momentum and stalls, it simply dips downward. This also tilts the aircraft into a brief shallow descent which prevents the main wing from stalling and maintains the craft's flying speed. This contrasts to the conventional main wing and rear empennage design wherein the plane may give a warning shudder before stalling and falling off on one wing. Still, a stall can be prevented if, at the first warning, you lower the nose and add power. On any aircraft it is of prime importance to maintain flying speed or be able to regain it quickly.

After running through a few basic maneuvers, you look down and get your bearings on the runway some distance

off to your left and far below. You review in your mind
how a proper landing should be made. You have learned
during training that ultralights fly a much lower and
tighter rectangular landing pattern than do heavier and
faster aircraft.

You ease the throttle off a bit and start your slow descent. Checking a leaning column of chimney smoke, you
determine the wind direction and approach the downwind
leg of the landing pattern from an angle.

You enter the pattern at an altitude of about two hundred feet, flying with the wind and parallel to the runway
several hundred yards off to your left. Peering at an angle
behind your left shoulder, you pick a point on the runway
where you intend to land. You keep it in mind, not in
sight, for you have quite a bit of flying still to do before
you reach the target spot.

Holding your altitude at two hundred feet, you make a
left turn into the base leg that approaches the runway at a
right angle. You throttle back a bit and start easing the
plane down, being careful to maintain proper flying speed.
You feel a slight crosswind buffet your craft, so you tilt
your wing into it to prevent being blown off course.

At an altitude of one hundred feet, and almost to the
point where you can look over your shoulder straight up

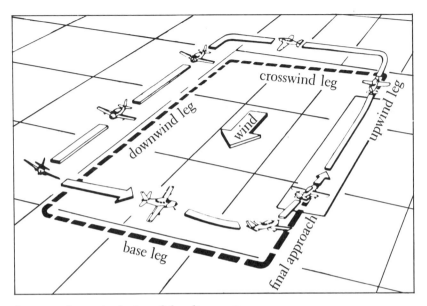

Layout of a typical aircraft landing pattern.

the runway, you make yet another left turn onto the final approach. The end of the runway and your intended landing spot lay straight ahead.

You ease off on the throttle a little more and adjust your low power glide just enough to maintain good flying speed. The Eagle has a L/D (lift-to-drag) ratio of about 7-to-1, enabling you to glide seven feet horizontally for every foot of lost altitude. You consider this as you judge the distance to your intended touchdown spot. As the ground comes toward you, you look up ahead, not down, and focus on your landing point.

Suddenly you start to sink too fast. You advance the throttle to regain speed and hold altitude, and cross over the end of the runway at what you judge to be an altitude of about thirty feet. You've allowed yourself plenty of room. In your view, your touchdown target is about where it belongs.

Although you feel sweat on your palms, you feel pretty good about everything so far. But the last twenty feet of altitude are the touchy ones. Suddenly you feel the air currents that are usually stronger the closer you get to the ground. For a brief moment you are not sure just which way to shift your weight. You hold steady, add a little throttle, and the ultralight rides through the temporary turbulence.

"Easy," you tell yourself. "Let her settle a little more. Relax."

Although the ground seems to be rushing up at you extra fast, you keep your steep glide. This is no place to be losing flying speed.

When you're about eight to ten feet from the ground, you shift back to bring the nose up a little and break your glide. You level off with barely enough speed to keep you in the air. In fact, for a startling moment you feel that you might lose your plane. Then, less than four feet above the runway you realize that you are in what is called ground effect. Air pressure under the plane builds up and causes a sensation of floating uncontrolled, like riding on a bubble. But you hold steady.

Throttled back, you concentrate on the last few feet of altitude, and on getting your wheels on the ground— softly.

Shifting your weight still farther back brings the nose up. The little plane flares, loses flying speed, and drops the last foot or so to the ground.

Flaring for a landing.

After rolling to a stop, you stifle the yelp of delight that rises in your throat. You are well aware that you are a long way from being a veteran pilot. You know there will be additional study sessions and more check flights under the watchful eye of your instructor before you dare even think of calling yourself an ultralight pilot.

Touchdown.

Since no official pilot's license is earned or required for ultralight flying, you may not even have any proof of your aerial prowess to hang on the wall or carry in your wallet. Yet, some instructors take care of this matter at the proper time by presenting students with their own personalized certificates of achievement.

But none of that really matters now. You are not looking for bonuses because you already have all the reward you need for the moment. You have just successfully completed your first real solo flight.

And now that the full realization of it strikes you again, the suppressed yelp of triumph slips its tether and bursts loudly from your throat.

Packing up for the day.

# 8. ULTRALIGHTS AT WORK AND PLAY

The world of ultralighting is rapidly expanding. More and more flyers, young and not so young, have completed both ground training and flight training. Given a clear, calm day, they buckle up, start their engines, and roar into the sky in search of fun and adventure.

The basic purpose of ultralight flying is for recreational fun. Most ultralighters are weekenders. They pack their ultralight on a trailer, or tie their dismantled machine to their cartop, and drive to some fairly isolated spot away from airports, air traffic corridors, and general congestion. During the calm morning hours they crisscross the skies within range of their fuel supplies. They practice take offs and landings. They explore and compare aerial adventures with one another. They simply enjoy themselves. This usually casual but thoroughly pleasant flying is the real basis of ultralighting.

Many flyers join such national organizations as the Experimental Aircraft Association (EAA) and the Aircraft

Ultralighting is primarily geared to the sheer fun and adventure of flying.

Owners and Pilots Association (AOPA) that have special ultralight divisions. (Their addresses are listed in the Further Information section.) Others join local groups and clubs of flying enthusiasts in order to share in the learning and the fun. A few inquiries provides any interested ultralighter with plenty of information about how and where to get started in ultralighting.

Often ultralighters take their dissembled aircraft along on their vacations. Nothing could be more colorful and dramatic than assembling your ultralight at the edge of Arizona's Monument Valley, then taking off and cruising around the spectacular up-thrusting red rock formations. What fun it is to putt-putt at low altitude over the brilliant foliage of New England, fly along the Mississippi River and wave at an amazed gathering of steamboat passengers, or skim the ocean waves. Indeed, the world is open to ultralighters who view it at a leisurely pace from a high angle.

You may add zest to your activities by going on cross-country flights. This offers you the opportunity to practice navigation. It requires that you plot your route carefully to be sure there is a chain of fuel stops lined along your path. It teaches you always to be alert to and respectful of the vagaries of wind and weather.

Skimming the waves in an ultralight.

Depending upon the machine and its fuel capacity, the range of an ultralight may vary from under a hundred miles to about two hundred miles. So a cross-country flight of appreciable length requires careful planning. Dedicated flyers have spanned the country from coast to coast and top to bottom. But most flying is done in short hops between cities or other less distant landmarks.

Ultralighters delight in staging fly-ins. Arriving from all directions and in all types of lightweight flying machines, you and other enthusiasts gather at some resort, usually adjacent to a flying field. You show off your machines, talk of adventures, and take to the air in spirited, competitive events.

A versatile trike may be used for ultralighting . . .

. . . or pontoon
boating (above) . . .

. . . or land
cruising (right).

You stage bomb drops, using water-filled balloons or paper bags of flour. From a designated altitude you try to hit the bull's-eye of a ground target.

You compete in climb-outs to see who can reach a specific altitude of, say, 1,000 feet the quickest from a standing start. The smallest pilot and the most powerful machine have an understandable advantage in this event.

You try deadstick spot landings—switching off your engine in midair, gliding down, and trying to touch down on or as near a target spot as you can.

Another event, called a rally, allows you to guess how much time it will take you to fly two laps around a marked-off course and land again at the starting point. Whoever touches down closest to his or her anticipated time wins. Naturally, you are not allowed to carry a watch!

There also may be a duration contest where you and another flyer are given a skimpy amount of fuel to put in your tanks, say about a quart. You take off together, climb until your engine coughs dead, then glide down for a landing. The last one to touch down wins.

In short, you do whatever you can think of to pit your flying skills against each other. Flying low and slow there is generally, if you have learned your lessons well, little risk involved.

Skis and warm clothes make winter ultralighting feasible.

Despite the aura of sheer fun that surrounds ultralighting activity, there are some who add more practical touches to their flying. Usually these are not business ventures, but private enterprises done for personal benefit. This is in keeping with the general ruling that ultralight activity must retain its flavor of recreation and sport.

There is nothing prohibitive, however, about an ultralighter reaping added benefits from his or her machine. A farmer or rancher finds an ultralight a very handy and inexpensive tool with which to patrol a fence line, survey a

An ultralight provides handy transportation to get around one's open land or farm.

flock of sheep, or, indeed, herd cattle. In range country, where distances are often vast, a rancher can use an ultralight as a quick and easy means to get from one part of the spread to another.

A farmer may take aerial photos of a grain field or orchard to check on the need for irrigation or perhaps detect from the air the first signs of insects or disease getting to his crop. Ultralights occasionally have been adapted to limited aerial spraying.

(Above)
An ultralight
can be used for
limited aerial
spraying.

(Right) A small aerial
spray-dispensing
unit.

Photographing from the open-air seat of an ultralight is easy, and often produces startlingly beautiful pictures. Of a less scenic nature, photographs can be used as an aid to mapping and surveying.

Although certain changes in the "recreational use only" rulings may need to be made, ultralighters are forever coming up with ideas by which their machines can be put to profitable use. Since it would be of commercial rather than recreational nature, such activity, however, should be limited to fully licensed pilots flying only FAA registered and certified ultralights.

Given proper approval, however, ultralights could well be used for all types of aerial inspections of such utilities as power lines or pipelines. They can be used in searching for seepage or debris in irrigation canals or water supply viaducts. Or they can patrol delta areas for leaks in dikes.

Already, on an informal basis, prospectors have used their ultralights to search out promising geological formations from aloft. Given a decent landing site, a prospector carrying a lightweight, portable sluice can reach in scant minutes places they might take a long day or more to reach on foot.

In both Israel and Saudi Arabia ultralights are being used during early stages of military flight training. Other foreign nations have purchased American-built ultralights for various sorts of patrol work, both military and civilian. Economy conscious governments everywhere are eyeing the ultralight to fill a variety of flying chores. A whole squadron of ultralights can be purchased and flown for less than the cost of a single helicopter. Everywhere, it seems, experimentation is going on in the area of the practical application for ultralight flying.

At this writing, several police departments in relatively small Southern Californian cities that cannot afford to purchase and operate half-million-dollar helicopters or fixed-wing airplanes are experimenting with ultralights for patrol work. In radio contact with ground patrols, such

Police departments are testing ultralights for use in aerial surveillance.

ultralights can combat crime by aiding in the apprehension of criminals. Widespread adoption of ultralights for surveillance and security appears inevitable.

With a little imagination, one can think of a hundred ways that the small aircraft can be put to practical, or, by special approval, even profitable use.

All together, and in light of the rapidly growing numbers of machines and flying enthusiasts, it appears certain that ultralights have established themselves firmly in the endless human quest for something that provides fun, adventure, and even practical use.

Ultralights are here, apparently, to stay.

# GLOSSARY

AGL— altitude above-ground-level.

ailerons—movable wing tabs that induce banked turns.

airspeed indicator (ASI)—an instrument that gauges speed in relation to the surrounding air.

altimeter—altitude indicator.

angle of attack—nose-up tilt of an aircraft.

axis—a straight, imaginary line around which an object rotates.

bungee—stretchable shock-absorbing cord used to tie some parts together.

camber—curvature of a wing from leading to trailing edge.

canard—a winglike stabilizing assembly mounted forward of the main wing.

center of gravity (CG)—a point at which the aircraft balances around all three axes.

Clear—standard warning call before starting engine. Or "Clear prop!"

cockpit—where the pilot sits.

control stick—a movable handle linked to elevator and ailerons to help control aircraft's flight. Also called *joystick*.

drag—friction. The force of resistance to movement through the air.

elevator—horizontal movable surface to control aircraft's pitch.

empennage—tail surfaces; generally rudder, stabilizer, and elevator.

engine—the aircraft's motor, or powerplant.

Federal Aviation Administration (FAA)—aviation's major, official controlling agency.

flare—to steepen the angle of attack during an aircraft's landing.

Flight Service Station (FSS)—a government facility to aid flyers, primarily with weather data and filing flight plans for cross-country trips.

gravity—the natural force that draws everything toward the earth's center.

joystick—see *control stick*.

kill switch—a convenient switch used to cut off engine power.

king post—a vertical staff protruding upward from the wing center, to which supporting cables are attached.

L/D—the ratio of lift to drag. Distance a plane can glide from a given altitude. 7 to 1 L/D means the aircraft can glide seven feet for every one foot of lost altitude.

lift—in aviation, the upward force generated by an aerodynamically shaped wing.

lock pin—see *safety*.

longitudinal axis—imaginary line running from front to rear of the aircraft.

main gear (mains)—the primary landing wheels.

mush—a nose-up attitude approaching a stall.

nosewheel—forward wheel of a tricycle landing gear.

pilotage—navigating by following a course of visual landmarks.

pitch—up-or-down movement of the nose of an aircraft.

powerplant—see *engine*.

preflight—careful inspection of the aircraft. Also called *walk-around*.

propeller (prop)—a revolving, thrust-producing bladed device.

Q-pin—quick-pin, safe pin, or lock pin. See *safety*.

recoil starter—a pull-cord engine starter.

rib—curved rod or structure that gives an aerodynamic shape to the wing.

roll—circular motion around the longtitudinal axis.

rpm—revolutions per minute.

rudder—a vertical moving surface to control yaw and help guide the aircraft.

ruddervator—combination rudder and elevator.

safety—self-locking keyring or safety-pin-like device for securing parts in place.

spar—the main wing member.

spoilerons—air-deflecting flaps on the wing that induce banked turns. Sometimes replace ailerons. Also called *spoilers*.

stabilizer—a rigid, generally horizontal winglike surface that helps steady the aircraft's flight.

stall—loss of wing lift.

stall speed—the speed at which an aircraft will cease to fly.

strut—a brace.

tachometer—engine-speed indicator.

tail skid—ground dragging part of some landing gears; also used to protect the empennage.

three axis controls—conventional aircraft stick-and-rudder pedal controls that operate ailerons, elevators, and rudder.

thrust—forward-directed force.

tricycle gear—three-wheel landing gear.

trike—self-contained unit made up of motor, landing gear, and cockpit.

ultralight—a class term for minimum-sized recreational aircraft. Generally used on powered craft, the description also applies to hang gliders.

ultralighting—the art of flying ultralight aircraft.

variable CG—to maintain balance by weight shifting.

variometer—rate-of-climb indicator.

vertical axis—imaginary line protruding straight up from the aircraft's center of gravity.

Vne—never-exceed-velocity, or maximum safe speed.

walkaround—preflight inspection.

weight-shift—see *variable CG*. Use of body weight movement to help control the aircraft.

yaw—side-to-side motion or waggle. Controlled with rudder.

# FOR FURTHER INFORMATION

BOOKS ON ULTRALIGHTING

*Ultralight Aircraft*, by Michael A. Markowski, Ultralight Publications, Hummelstown, PA, 1982

*31 Practical Ultralight Aircraft You Can Build*, by Don Dwiggins, TAB Books, Inc., Blue Ridge Summit, PA, 1980

*The Ultralight Aviator's Handbook*, Flight Patterns, Tempe, AZ 85292

*Aeronautics for Powered Ultralight*, by Steven Hanes & R. Cipriano, Wing Publications, P.O. Box 25996, Tempe, AZ 85292

*Ultralight Airmanship*, by Jack Lambie, Ultralight Publications, Hummelstown, PA, 1982

*Powered Ultralight Training Course*, by Dennis Pagen, Dennis Pagen, Pub., P.O. Box 601, State College, PA 16801, 1981

MAGAZINES

*Glider Rider* (monthly), P.O. Box 6009, Chattanooga, TN 37401

*Ultralight* (monthly), Experimental Aircraft Association (EAA), P.O. Box 229, Hales Corners, WI 53130

*Ultralight Pilot* (bimonthly), Aircraft Owners & Pilots Association (AOPA), P.O. Box 5800, Bethesda, MD 20814

*Ultralight Aircraft* (bimonthly), P.O. Box 28897, San Diego, CA 92127

# INDEX

Boldface indicates illustration

## About the Author

Charles (Chick) Coombs graduated from the University of California, at Los Angeles, and decided at once to make writing his career. While working at a variety of jobs, he labored at his typewriter early in the morning and late at night. An athlete at school and college, Mr. Coombs began by writing sports fiction. He soon broadened his interests, writing adventure and mystery stories, and factual articles as well. When he had sold over a hundred stories, he decided to try one year of full-time writing, chiefly for young people, and the results justified the decision.

Eventually he turned to writing books. To date, he has published more than seventy books, both fiction and nonfiction, covering a wide range of subjects, from aviation, space, and oceanography, to drag racing, motorcycling, and other sports.

Mr. Coombs and his wife, Eleanor, live in Westlake Village, near Los Angeles.